MIXED UP

COCKTAIL RECIPES (AND FLASH FICTION) FOR
THE DISCERNING DRINKER (AND READER)

EDITED BY
NICK MAMATAS AND **MOLLY TANZER**

Skyhorse Publishing

Skyhorse Publishing books may be purchased in bulk at special discounts for sales promotion, corporate gifts, fund-raising, or educational purposes. Special editions can also be created to specifications. For details, contact the Special Sales Department, Skyhorse Publishing, 307 West 36th Street, 11th Floor, New York, NY 10018 or info@skyhorsepublishing.com.

Skyhorse® and Skyhorse Publishing® are registered trademarks of Skyhorse Publishing, Inc.®, a Delaware corporation.

Visit our website at www.skyhorsepublishing.com.

10 9 8 7 6 5 4 3 2 1

Library of Congress Cataloging-in-Publication Data is available on file.

Cover design by Jenny Zemanek
Cover images courtesy of iStockphoto

Print ISBN: 978-1-5107-1803-6
Ebook ISBN: 978-1-5107-1804-3

Printed in China

MIXED UP

Contents

· ·

Around the World in a Daze: Drinking Everywhere

Day Drinking: The Editors' Inspiration

Introduction

· ·

by Molly Tanzer

"Nothing Gold"

HOW DOES ONE PROPERLY DRINK a cocktail? The answer seems obvious—through the teeth, past the gums, and all that—but you'd be surprised. People do it wrong literally all the time. Go to any bar or party and you'll see people idling over their drinks, unaware that as they dawdle the botanicals are withering, the oils are settling, the glass and its contents are warming unpleasantly.

The temptation to linger over a drink is understandable. A well-crafted cocktail seems like something to savor. Additionally, company is most pleasant when people are just lubricated enough, and hastily pounding cocktails can prematurely end a fun evening. Pragmatically speaking, when one spends money in the liquor store on an esoteric ingredient, or forks over fifteen dollars in a bar for one drink, it feels rash to just gulp down one's classic Fin de Siècle or "modern take" on an Old Fashioned.

And yet, that is *exactly* what you should do. You'll enjoy your drink more, and you won't insult your bartender or host if you knock back their creations. In fact, they will appreciate your appreciation of the necessarily ephemeral nature of their work. Neither should you worry that you won't get the full experience of the drink by sipping lively. In doing so, you will taste more, appreciate more. Nothing gold can stay, and that applies to leaves, Eden, the dawn . . . and *cocktails*.

Unfortunately, the slow sipping of a cocktail is too often a fossilized error. We're trained to go slow, to pace ourselves*. And that is *exactly* why, as an enthusiastic home bartender, I'm proud to present you with *Mixed Up*. Part mixology guide, part anthology, *Mixed Up* is a sophisticated mélange of the coldest drinks and the hottest voices writing today. It pairs sensual stories with bewitching recipes, demonstrating time and again that quick delights need not be hurried; that luxuriating doesn't necessarily mean languishing. I believe these brief stories will satisfy your senses as richly as any longer tale—and if you accompany each with its associated cocktail, you'll come around to the fine art of briskly consuming the beautiful.

Every cocktail has a story. Sometimes it's literally literary, like the appearance of the Vesper in a James Bond novel. Sometimes it's the sort of story you can casually relate to your party guests while you serve them, such as explaining who invented the Josie Russell, and why the original is so sour. Well, in this book, every story has a cocktail. Sweet or bitter, pleasant or shocking, you won't soon forget them. And really, if there's anything more suitable to cocktail party talk than the new author you just discovered, I'm not sure what it might be!

—Molly Tanzer,
Longmont, Colorado
January 2017

---

* Pacing yourself is, naturally, an excellent idea while drinking, but we recommend a glass of water in between drinks, rather than letting them go warm.

Introduction

. . . .

by Nick Mamatas

"Have You Heard the One About . . ."

R EAD ANY GOOD SHORT STORIES lately? Probably not. Maybe there's a well-worn copy of *Nine Stories* on your shelves.
Perhaps you flip through the *New Yorker* every week and
sometimes, *sometimes*, your eyes idle on a page full of well-observed
description and telling details. There's a possibility that you have
downloaded a short fiction app onto your smartphone, and when
the subway is stuck in a tunnel between stations for an hour and
Facebook has exhausted itself, your thumb finds it.

Heard any good short stories lately? Of course you have. The
world is made of them. The scripts of your favorite TV show episodes
are twenty-two or forty-eight pages long. Every joke is a little story;
so is every mouthful of juicy, acid gossip; so is every viral meme.
"So," your online date says from across the table at a bar close to your
apartment—the location chosen in case things go very poorly, or
very well—"I've read your profile, but tell me about yourself." And
you do, and now you're the storyteller.

Some of the best short stories ever told were shared over
cocktails. Social lubricant plus sensory stimulation plus company

is the formula for a tale worth remembering. And then came a terrible interregnum and both the short story and the cocktail all but vanished. The slick magazines replaced their monthly fiction features with more ads, and a generation decided to consume sugary concoctions and novelty shots instead of real drinks. The 1990s were terrible, and the 2000s were worse, for everything.

The cocktail has finally emerged from the darkness, thanks partially to quality bitters becoming widely available again, and partially to leading bars and restaurants making a cocktail menu a focus. But whither short fiction?

I've always loved short stories, and there are a handful of classics we all know—"Araby", "The Lottery", "The Tell-Tale Heart"—but what about new stories, from writers who are alive, and who like a drink now and again (but I repeat myself). The same requirements are necessary: new ingredients, and new advocates.

There's something perverse about wanting to work with short fiction. While there are plenty of stories being written—mostly by students, as études—and a determined if not exactly vibrant small press in which to publish some of them, short fiction hasn't made its comeback yet. Literary journals nobody reads, run by editors publishing their friends and colleagues, primarily showcase tales of infidelity in the faculty lounge and epiphanies over teacups, just as they did a century ago. Genre fiction is in better shape, but those magazines are still chock-full of the usual tropes—lonely spacemen slowly going mad aboard malfunctioning starships, alcoholic cops fretting over the corpse of a dead girl. And as it turns out, the narrator was the corpse all along.

So why *not* put excellent short stories in a book of cocktail recipes, to be nonchalantly discovered in the Food/Beverage section of your local enormous chain store instead of the Fiction section—just as fiction routinely took its place alongside nonfiction in newspapers and magazines? Why not *mix up* literary fiction, fantasy, crime, romance, and absurdist literature—like in the "all-story" periodicals of the golden age? Most cocktails are meant to be swigged, so let us clutch our glasses and quickly upend their contents down our very throats, because the time has come and we mean fucking business.

This is that moment. These stories are here to be gulped. I am already drunk on them. You are next.

—Nick Mamatas
Berkeley, California
January 2017

Cheap Dates:
Booze You Can Use!

Some of the classic cocktails that we all know and love.

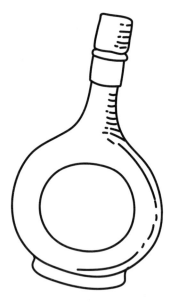

Eat the Wyrm

by Elizabeth Hand

J OHAN HAD BEEN TELLING ME about Solopgang ever since I arrived in Greenland.

"It's not on the way to anyplace, so you have to make a special pilgrimage. Maybe we can go after the SIKON conference."

Nothing's on the way to anyplace in Greenland, I wanted to say, but what was the point? Solopgang was legendary in the way things are, or used to be, in Greenland—famous to fifteen people. The name was Danish for "sunrise." The guy who ran it, Kurt Gunderson, had knocked around the country for a few years as a corporate geologist before lighting out for the territory and, in one of the country's more improbable reinventions, becoming a grower and distiller of mescal.

I'm not much of a drinker, but I used to have a taste for tequila. Not a very elevated taste—Cuervo Gold was about as far as it reached. But after the SIKON conference, where I spent three futile days discussing core samples and how to downplay the dangers of nuclear contamination as the ice sheet melted, exposing the waste stored there decades earlier, I was ready for a pilgrimage.

LET'S GO, I texted Johan.

He picked me up on Friday. It took us three days to reach Ipatkitak, on the northeast coast. We stayed in rentals the first two nights, corrugated buildings that in the US might have been used for storing cannibalized lawnmowers or refrigerators too heavy to be lugged to the dump. The morning of the third day we left our SUV in the lee of an immense spar of black rock, and hiked the remainder of the way.

The views were spectacular, black crags and that endless stretch of indigo water, the luminous cerulean of melting icebergs igniting to gold as the sun rose, the blue heart of a dying flame. The air had a raw, stony smell I've only experienced in the Greenland wilderness, untainted by the stink of fuel and rotting fish and burning tires that hangs over the larger settlements; a stink recently grown more corrosive as reps from corporations and nations crowded the villages in the grab for mineral rights as the icecap disappeared.

"Can't we just stay here?" I asked on the third night, when we pitched a tent beneath the rusting hulk of an abandoned transport vehicle.

"Maybe Kurt will let us stay with him." Johan rolled over in his sleeping bag, opened the tent flap so he could light a cigarette. "We can tend his greenhouse."

"Greenland greenhouse. That's an oxymoron."

Johan nodded. "Oxymoron would have been a good name for the bar."

During the Cold War, Ipatkitak had been the site of a small US air base. Military detritus was everywhere, strewn across the barren rocks like the wreckage of some long-ago plane crash. Shattered windshields, husks of Jeeps and trailers, tires as big as a wading pool. Kurt's homestead was still half a day's trek from here. We left early the next morning and arrived before noon, just as a cold fog settled in, obscuring the surrounding plain and the distant sweep of jagged mountains.

"Welcome!"

Kurt strode from a small Quonset hut that appeared to float on the rocky plain, a black bubble. He was short for a Dane, dark-haired, not blond, with a graying beard and round tinted eyeglasses. He looked like a benign if earnest Trotskyite. "Johan, great to see you! And Emma, so glad we finally meet. Come, you can put your things inside, then we can head over to Solopgang. It's only a minute's walk that way."

He gestured vaguely at the thickening fog as we followed him into the Quonset hut. Half an hour later, we ventured back out. I'd been hoping to fortify myself with some food before we turned to the business of sampling Kurt's booze, but Johan was too impatient.

"We've come eight hundred miles for a drink. I want that drink."

Kurt nodded, and we followed him to another Quonset hut, smaller, its round windows brilliantly lit from within. Solar panels and propane tanks and several generators littered the rocky ground. A polar bear hide dangled from a flagpole, its jaws rattling in the wind. Above the hut's entrance hung a hand-carved wooden sign, the letters picked out in crimson paint.

SOLOPGANG

Kurt held the door for us as we stepped inside, blasted by a wave of heat so intense that immediately I began to sweat. I blinked, blinded by banks of growlights suspended from the domed ceiling and arranged along the perimeter of the space. I felt as though we'd stepped onstage, at the mercy of hundreds of spotlights, or into the loading bay of a UFO.

"My god, Emma, look at all this!" Johan cried.

The room was filled with huge, spiky plants, some nearly as tall as I was, their thick, blade-shaped leaves shading from periwinkle blue to a green so rich and dark the leaves might have been carved from malachite. I inhaled deeply, my nostrils stung by the heat and also the slightly acrid scent of the agave plants; it was as though their leaves had been singed.

I turned to Kurt, who had stopped to stroke a long stalk that held a creamy agave blossom. "How can you possibly keep them warm enough in winter?"

He shrugged. "That's my secret, right? But very strange things are happening around here. Everywhere, I think. Did you hear they found an arm on the Garm glacier? Thousands of years old, they think, like the Ice Man. Tattoos on the hand and part of a sleeve made from sealskin. But only the arm. What do you think happened to the rest of him?"

I laughed. "They'll find him when the rest of the glacier melts."

"No, the ice everywhere near him is gone. They searched and searched and they found nothing. I think something ate him. Okay, this way."

I'd expected Solopgang to bear at least a cursory resemblance to an actual bar or restaurant. While it didn't cost as much as climbing Everest, or dinner at a Michelin-starred place, I'd heard you could rack up a hefty bar tab.

But the space Kurt ushered us into was a narrow annex with walls of unpainted plywood. The cement floor was sticky. There were no windows. Strings of white LEDs drooped from nails in the wood, illuminating a rectangular table with a battered red formica top, and six metal folding chairs. Beside the door someone had scrawled on a piece of cardboard with a Sharpie.

Eat the wyrm.

"Have a seat," said Kurt. He walked to a small metal cabinet, opened it, and withdrew a bottle and three glass tumblers. "We'll start with this."

"No." Johan shook his head, then pointed at the sign by the door. "We want to taste it."

Kurt hesitated, set the bottle and tumblers back on the shelf and walked toward us, pulling out a mobile. Johan did the same with his phone. After a brief exchange of information and shadow currency, Kurt nodded.

"Right back," he said, and headed into the greenhouse. I sat on one of the rickety chairs next to Johan.

"I've never done that," I said, staring at the hand-lettered sign. "Eat the worm. Have you?"

"Yeah, sure. It's not a big deal—in Mexico, they eat caterpillars, you know? This is very different. Five K it cost, but it'll be worth it."

A few minutes later Kurt returned. He settled at the table, and placed two small bottles in front of us, each stoppered with a cork. Carefully he removed the corks.

"There you go," he said.

At first I thought they were made of the same kind of glass they used for old Coke bottles, that diffuse green-blue color that always reminded me of a hurricane sky.

But when I gingerly picked up mine, I saw that the glass was clear. The strange glaucous hue came from the liquid inside. Something floated at the bottom of the glass.

No, didn't float—swam. I gazed at it, my neck prickling: a creature roughly the size and length of my pinkie finger, shimmering and pulsating, its sinuous motion causing it to flicker dull orange, then the brilliant acid green of Vasoline glass.

I drew the bottle closer to my face, hardly daring to breathe. The little creature writhed, coiling and uncoiling so that it was difficult to count its legs. *Four*, I thought. A rippling scarlet fringe surrounded its thumbnail-sized head, the same color as its eyes. There were three of them.

I glanced at Johan. He'd already brought the glass to his lips, eyes shining and his cheeks pink with excitement.

"Skol," he said, raising his tumbler to me and downing the mescal in a gulp. I watched him, my mouth dry, as he and Kurt both turned to me expectantly. I drew the bottle to my lips, caught a faint odor of sulfur and an even fainter hint of putrefying meat. I closed my eyes.

"Skol," I said, and drank.

Margarita

WHAT COULD BE MORE CLASSIC than a margarita? Unfortunately, like most classics in any genre, its ubiquity means most interpretations are abominable; the potently potable equivalent of reading *Romeo and Juliet* as a romance instead of as a tragic tale of two thoughtless teenagers who get half their families killed over a crush. Anyway, while I'm not against variations on a theme—a tavern near my pad serves up legitimately great margs that utilize sweet and sour mix, are served in a pint glass, and are awesome—there's something to be said about more elegant, simple interpretations of the margarita. When it comes to cocktails, it's rarely the wrong choice to serve up delicious ingredients in rational proportions, so spring for the Cointreau over Triple Sec; get a nice tequila.

Ingredients

1½ oz. reposado tequila

¾ oz. Cointreau

½ a juicy lime (or an entire one if it's drier)

1 tsp. agave nectar

2 dashes orange bitters

How to Make It: The method of the margarita is also straightforward: shake all the ingredients with lots of cracked ice until cold; serve in a chilled cocktail glass, no garnish. Lime wheels or wedges just fall in people's faces, and no one needs that kind of hassle.

Speaking of variations on a theme, remember: tequila never contains a worm, but many types of mescal—*mescal con gusano*—do. You can use mescal in a margarita; it has a smokier, richer taste that can be quite a revelation, but mescal and tequila are not the same spirit at all. I personally prefer tequila in a margarita because I like the clean, freshness of the drink, but play around with it and see what you prefer!

Cuba Libre

THE CLASSIC RUM AND COKE may not be fancy, but it is delicious. There's just something magical about the way the fizzy mysterious sweetness of Coke, the sourness of the lime, and the buttery, molasses notes of rum come together. Again, as with most classics, my advice is to keep it simple. Get so-called "Mexican Coke," made the proper way, with sugarcane. Use a decent golden rum, not a white or a spiced rum. Squeeze in the lime, incorporating it into the drink; don't just hang it off the edge of the glass like a misplaced apostrophe.

The first rum and Coke I ever had was made for me by the man I would one day marry (and divorce, but let's stay focused on the positive). He came to visit me when I was working on campus one summer, staying in the dorms, and brought with him a pound bag of limes, a handle of Mount Gay rum, and two two-liter bottles of Coke. "What's all this?" I asked. "Things that I need," he replied, and mixed me one before taking me to bed. They say taste and smell are the most powerful memory triggers, and maybe it's true—whenever I drink one, I'm nineteen again, sitting on the porch of my dorm, wondering what the hell I'm getting into.

Ingredients
2 oz. golden rum
Lime wedge
Coca-Cola Classic

How to Make It: Pour rum into a highball glass and squeeze in juice of a lime wedge. Fill glass with ice, top with Coca-Cola, then run the lime around the edge of the glass and toss in. My ex-husband would insist you must stir the drink with a finger to get it just right, but I'd suggest a swizzle unless you're exceptionally intimate with your guests.

Wes Anderson
Uses a Urinal

by Jarett Kobek

I WAS AT MUSSO & Frank, the oldest restaurant in Hollywood, with my friend Thomas. We were there because I was moving back to Los Angeles and I had to come down for a week to get some things in order. Thomas had moved to LA a few months earlier—I'd known him forever—and he'd allowed me to crash on his couch while I ran around the city, dealing with address changes and my new landlord.

I'd been the one to suggest that we go to Musso.

"What's that?" he'd asked.

"It's this old restaurant, all wood, it's where the shittiest B-listers hang out. You can always see some old hack from some old sitcom. Kenneth Anger took me a few times. We'll get drunk."

That's how I found myself at the bar of Musso & Frank, throwing back champagne cocktails. I'm an idiot who only has the memory for one drink, so I always order the last drink I've seen someone else order, and the last drink I'd seen someone else order was a champagne cocktail. So, champagne cocktail.

With the first drink, I experienced vague waves of menace, something that happens with every substance of merit. I attribute this to my first drug experiences being heavy doses of LSD, which wired my brain to produce a terrible expectation. Whatever the drug. Alcohol included.

"I've got to go to the bathroom," I said.

I tried to use the urinal, but I couldn't use the urinal because I was too anxious and there was too much noise in the bathroom with other people coming in and going out and talking to each other.

For me, anyway, urinal use requires silence.

I stopped trying to use the urinal. I went into one of the toilets. I wondered if I should feel humiliated about being the kind of man who drinks fruity drinks and then can't use a urinal.

But I decided it didn't matter. My life was falling apart. I was moving to Los Angeles. There are worse things in the world than not being able to use a urinal.

Back at the bar, Thomas had ordered us another round. Somewhere halfway into the second drink, my anxiety disappeared. Now I was fine. Now I was tight.

That's when I noticed Thomas staring at the entrance. There was a group of people waiting to be seated, including: (1) The actor Jeff Goldblum, who looked exactly like the actor Jeff Goldblum. (2) A woman in her late 20s, wearing a reasonably interesting party dress. (3) The cinematic auteur Wes Anderson, who was sporting a green corduroy jacket.

"Oh, yeah," I said. "Wes Anderson."

"What?" asked Thomas.

"Wes Anderson," I said. "In the green jacket. You know, Wes Anderson?"

"I know Wes Anderson," said Thomas. "But I had no idea what Wes Anderson looks like. I was looking at the chick."

"Didn't you notice Jeff Goldblum?"

"Jeff Goldblum?" asked Thomas.

"Girl," I said, "you need glasses."

"Wait," said Thomas. "Why in God's name do you know what Wes Anderson looks like?"

"The Internet, okay," I said. "The Internet."

The staff seated Wes Anderson and Jeff Goldblum by the far wall in one of the booths. Our backs were to them but I could see the cohort, kind of, in the mirror above the bar. I finished my drink and ordered a third.

"How much do you think these things cost, anyway?" I asked.

"Too much," said Thomas. "This joint is high-class, brother. They got genuine film directors and actors from the TV and everything."

"I forget," I said. "Don't you like Wes Anderson?"

"Sort of," said Thomas. "I liked *Rushmore* and *The Royal Tenenbaums*."

"What about *The Darjeeling Limited*?"

"I didn't see it," said Thomas.

"No one likes that movie," I said. "No one but me. Even the stupid short film before it. It's grotesque. It's so woman-hating and self-pitying. But I liked that too. Plus, Natalie Portman kicks off her knickers."

"What?" asked Thomas.

There wasn't much to talk about with Wes Anderson in the room. I was thinking about how I'd seen this British film *Submarine*, which was a British coming of age thing directed by a comedian named Richard Ayoade. He'd stolen Wes Anderson's entire toolbox.

All the tricks and techniques you'd associate with a film by Wes Anderson, all the flat space, the handmade art, the slow motion, the snap zooms. It was all in *Submarine* and done so much better than in any of the films of Wes Anderson.

There was an entire generation of kids coming into film school—if kids still cared about film in the twenty-first century, which maybe they didn't—for who Wes Anderson wasn't a contemporary director. I'd been nineteen and in college when *Rushmore* came out, but that was sixteen years prior. So there were all these kids, kids in their twenties, who hadn't watched Wes Anderson develop as a filmmaker, but had woken up into an aesthetic reality where Wes Anderson was an established master of a certain empty style. I had been living in a world where Wes Anderson was a new commodity, a promising talent, but in these kids' world, Wes Anderson was a fixed planetary being, a person who could be counted upon to show up in green jackets and shoot a slow motion take of some sexually arrested men walking in a hallway while The Kinks' "Muswell Hillbillies" plays on the nondiegetic soundtrack. Theirs was the real world, not mine, a world where the Wes Anderson toolbox was so apparent that Richard Ayoade could steal it wholesale and make a much better film than Wes Anderson had ever made.

When the fuck did I get so old.

"I tried to read the book that *Submarine* was based on," I said. "But it was really fucking disturbing, actually. It was full of all this pedophilia. So I stopped after about thirty pages. That's not what the movie is like."

"Wait," said Thomas. "What's *Submarine*?"

"Weren't we just talking about *Submarine*?"

"No?"

"Oh," I said.

Wes Anderson was in the mirror.

"Speaking of pedophilia," I said, "did you watch *Moonrise Kingdom*? There's some very creepy lingering shots of an artfully posed twelve-year-old."

"That fucking movie," said Thomas. "It's the twee-est thing ever made. The only way I could have experienced anything more twee is if Zooey Deschanel was playing the ukulele and squirting in my face."

"I saw it in Rhode Island," I said. "And you know it was shot in Newport. And you know Rhode Islanders, they'll go see anything that has even the most tangential relationship with the state. So I saw it at the Avon on Thayer Street, and there was a moment, I kid you not, where a group of people recognized a shooting location, which was an empty field somewhere in Middletown. And so they all started cheering. A bunch of Rhode fucking Islanders cheering a field."

"Do you want another?" asked Thomas.

I was looking at Wes Anderson and Jeff Goldblum and that woman's modestly fascinating party dress. And then I noticed that Wes Anderson was standing up, getting out of their booth.

"Here's your chance," I said.

"My chance?"

"Here's your chance to see if the man who directed *Moonrise Kingdom* uses urinals. Is he too twee for the urinal? Only you can find out."

"What?"

"Wes Anderson is going to the bathroom. You should follow him and see if he uses the urinal."

"I'm not doing that," said Thomas. "I'm not going to go watch Wes Anderson use a urinal."

"You son of a bitch," I said.

"Fine," I said.

"I'll do it," I said.

I was very drunk but I was okay, I wasn't reeling. I've only reeled once and that was back before the wide release of *Rushmore*.

I followed Wes Anderson as he made his way to the back of the restaurant, staring into the green corduroy of his jacket, wondering yet again about my life choices.

After he pushed open the bathroom door, I waited a bit, waited so that it wouldn't seem so obvious.

And then I went into the bathroom.

And there he was. There Wes Anderson was.

And he was using a urinal.

He was using the urinal that I had tried to use and couldn't.

The director of *Moonrise Kingdom* was using a urinal.

Champagne Cocktail

CHAMPAGNE IS ONE OF MY favorite drinks, and it's definitely my favorite wine. I adore it on its own, but I also like how it plays with others. Obviously, as there are two cocktails and a punch that utilize the bubbly in this book. My house, my rules!

The beauty of the classic champagne cocktail is that it improves both the fancy stuff and less refined expressions of sparkling wine by adding both sweetness and bitterness. Just make sure you choose a brut bubbly. You are adding an entire sugar cube! I tend to go with a nicer prosecco spumante or a cava if I'm not going for real champagne.

Ingredients
Sugar cube
Angostura bitters
Brut Champagne (or a less sweet sparkling wine)

How to Make It: Put a sugar cube into a champagne flute. Saturate—yes, *saturate*—said cube with Angostura bitters, then top slowly with champagne. The champagne will foam and fizz a lot more because of the bitters and sugar, so take your time. Do not stir. The drink will naturally become sweeter as you drink it; that's part of the charm.

Good old Angostura aromatic bitters. They're like Michael Caine: in everything, and they make everything a bit better for it.

Angostura aromatic bitters enhance the flavors of alcohol with subtle, indeed *aromatic* notes of spice and medicine and sweetness. What's in them? Well, who knows? Some gentian, definitely. That's on the label. Caramel color, and "natural flavorings," too. No bark from the Angostura tree, queerly enough . . . though whether it contains some sort of extract or essence of said bark, no one except the makers themselves know for sure.

Regardless of what they may or may not contain, they're essential to any home bartender. That said, if you'd like to read more about the bizarre and bizarrely litigious history of Angostura aromatic bitters, check out Amy Stewart's essential *The Drunken Botanist*.

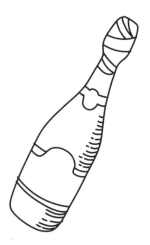

The End of the
End of History

by Nick Mamatas

THE YEAR 2000 WASN'T ACTUALLY the beginning of the new millennium, but it was the beginning of the end of good house parties in the East Village. The 1990s were puffy weed, Tecate, and spontaneous make-out sessions between girls with buzzcuts and once-broken noses. Relationships blossomed from meet-cute to total screaming destruction over the course of forty minutes. Space-time hypercompressed, like a party of ninety people rotating in and out of a three-hundred-square-foot apartment. *Everyone* showed up eventually.

Then, dot-coms. Remember Beenz and Boo and people who'd call themselves "millionaires on paper" with smiles on their faces? Happy smiles, not the coprophagous grins they all wore one year later, when Silicon Valley imploded. Sure is cute when everyone realizes that they'd believed their own lies, right?

I was living in a closet in a three-bedroom railroad on Avenue B. Sounds terrible, but rent was just four hundred bucks. My roommate Zachariah, one of the "bedroom boys" at six hundred fifty a month, made it big. His conspiracy theory website had been acquired by

PolyVerse Media for no reason anyone could explain. Something something functionality solutions for content-portal verticals.

Zachariah's new friends mustered in the living room. They stood out because their shirts were ironed, and they manifested tight single-sex knots around any woman who failed to walk in on a man's arm. Jacqueline, who rented our couch for two seventy-five, performed mixology. She had commandeered the coffee table and sat behind it like the Buddha. Not a beer can to be seen; we were all moving up in the world.

Even in a tenement party, there are silences when a dozen conversations die at once, and the CD just happens to end. That night when the moment struck, only one of us was out of sync. Zachariah's new boss, Pasquale.

"This is not a martini," Pasquale said. Then he shouted, "There is no such thing as a vodka martini!"

It wasn't clear whom he was addressing. The girl next to him was clutching a martini glass, but Pasquale was holding one too. He might have been talking to *the drink itself*, like a madman, like Vincent van Gogh bellowing imprecations into the bloodied ear in his palm.

A murmur arose, but not fast enough to drown out Jacqueline's response. She peered up at Pasquale with infinite compassion, and like the Buddha, said, "Screw you."

Pasquale said, "Look it up. A 'vodka martini' is nothing but a kangaroo cocktail. It wasn't even called a martini til the 1950s, when suburbanites started pouring any old spirit into martini glasses. Web answer dot com, have you heard of it?"

And that was it. I didn't drink. I smoked pot, so I perceived it first, at that moment, years before anyone else. The end of conversation, of enthusiastic guessing—the death of interpretation and variation. Every fact in the universe known, and no room for anything but known facts. Pasquale knew. Jacqueline, despite her bartending school certificate and fast hands and a head of black hair to make a corvid jealous, did not.

"The vermouth I am using is of the highest quality," Jacqueline said.

"It doesn't matter," Pasquale said. Pasquale sported a sort of enforced baldness; his hairline was obviously receding, so he just shaved everything to try and hide it. His head was practically glowing with hot blood. I cast around for Zachariah and our eyes met. He was a goner in the far corner, unblinking, face bleached.

"You called this a martini," Pasquale said. Jacqueline looked ready to jump over the coffee table and eat his face. Who insults their bartender? Who insults their *female* bartender? Someone so unfathomably, stupidly rich that he was going to get laid no matter what he said or did.

My senses heightened, I heard something over the susurrus of the ruined party. The apartment was a fifth-story walk-up. Our ceiling was the roof, and something had just thumped on it.

"Language is a tool of communication," Jacqueline said. "Prescriptivism is dead. You're just conserving a linguistic custom by proscribing use of 'martini' to describe drinks lacking . . . berry juice. You want your berry juice, little boy, I understand. But as you said, it's been fifty years of vodka martinis. If custom prevails, it is my custom that is prevailing, for the tools of production are mine."

It got *very* grad school very quickly. There was a knock on the door and I snaked my way over to it.

"So if I were to pour some wingnuts into a martini glass and then smear the rim of the glass with vermouth, that too would be a martini?" Pasquale demanded to know. "A wingnut martini!"

Through the peephole I saw a face like a distorted Thom York. I hurriedly opened up.

"Vladimir Putin," I said. His bodyguard, approximately the size of a glacier, brushed past me, and Vladimir Putin followed, shrugging his suit jacket off into my arms. He was on vacation. *Kursk*, that doomed submarine, was trapped under five hundred million tons of ocean, and the Russian president was here.

By the time Putin hit the living room, his tie was undone, his sleeves rolled up. Putin, Russian president. Putin, judo brown belt. Putin, still in power to this day. He is an old man now, and I am not a kid anymore. I quit smoking—I started drinking again the morning after the party.

Putin had a martini glass in his hand. I did the math. Jacqueline was out; it had to have been Pasquale's, freshly liberated. He swallowed in a practiced gulp and declared, backed by 4,600 nuclear warheads, "This is quite good. Vodka and what else?" His English was unaccented, wiped clean by KGB training.

"Several molecules of vermouth," Pasquale said. "But it's *not* a martini."

Vladimir Putin glanced at his bodyguard and tensed his free hand into a fist. Pinned to the far wall, Zachariah fainted but did not hit the ground.

Jacqueline pierced two olives with a toothpick and offered them up.

Dirty Martini

I LOVE A DIRTY VODKA martini. Even though I'm a big gin drinker I just don't care for it in combination with vermouth (also an herbal, complex flavor) whether the finished drink is served with a twist, or especially with olive brine. As I think the dirty martini is the finest expression of the martini, I'm recommending it here to establish it as a classic, a bold act of cocktail advocacy, I know. But I mean, people will harp on the gin thing, just like in our accompanying story, so, my work is clearly cut out for me.

People make a big deal over the apparent issue of including vermouth in martinis, too; they take a lot of pride in dissing it wholesale, or buy atomizers to gingerly spray it over the surface of chilled spirit. As always, I say make drinks as you like them, but I'm also a huge booster of vermouth—especially these days, when there are so many delicious varieties. Sure, bargain basement vermouth is gross, but with notable exceptions most bottom-shelf liquor is pretty gross. One uses so little vermouth per drink, it just makes sense to go for nicer stuff that will enhance your drink. (Get nice olives, too!)

Ingredients

2 oz. vodka

½ oz. dry vermouth

1 tsp. to 1 tbsp. olive brine (however salty you like it)

Green olives, to garnish

How to Make It: Build drink in a shaker (sans olives), then stir vigorously with lots of cracked ice. Sure, you *can* shake a martini, as "bruising" gin is a myth—but shaking any drink including vermouth will produce a cloudy cocktail, and in this case, it will also result in a drink that is more watery. Try it both ways and see what you prefer. Anyway, strain into a chilled cocktail glass; garnish with as many olives as you like. I nearly always do two.

I've Been Tired

· ·

by Cara Hoffman

I WAS LIVING BY THE inlet between a hobo jungle and a family who used their money to keep two acres of Christmas decorations lit all year long.

The sky above the town was a blank white gray, and dusk descended in the evenings all at once like a storm coming on.

My child worked for a toymaker sanding tiny wooden pigs, and feeding the man's sheep, and I worked mowing lawns for a turf grass research facility.

In the evenings we played rummy and drank Negronis.

Children are partial to Negronis as they taste like medicine, and because one of the main ingredients is made from crushed insects. Children shouldn't be served more than a teaspoon or two of the drink, but there's no reason not to teach them how to mix one properly.

My child could make a good Negroni. He had the right proportions of Campari and gin down, and was fond of experimenting with orange peel.

Cocktail hour for the family of two in what passed for rural America in the early aughts involved crackers, a couple Negronis, and a couple ginger ale and bitters. It was a time to deconstruct our surreal surroundings, strategize an escape plan, listen to the Pixies, and sew sock puppets.

The name of the road we lived on had the word "extension" at the end of it. It crossed a little stream then came to a junction marked with a crooked street sign that read, I swear to Christ, PODUNK. Just behind the Podunk sign was a flagpole flying the Confederate flag, and behind that was a swing set, a septic tank, and a trailer.

The people who moved to the town to escape various failures and set up various cottage industries with their family money were breathless about the possibility of slow culture and a new life as part of "the community." They could buy eggs from their neighbors.

The child and I didn't fit in. It rained four days a week, people went missing, meth labs caught fire. The back-to-the-landers and city-born life-stylers were either drunks, pathologically interested in Tibet, or Harvard-educated dirt farmers who were starry-eyed that at last they could hold a baby chick in their very own hands. My child was briefly friends with a child of the Harvard farmers. That kid could not wipe his own ass until he was six years old.

Women in yoga pants speed-walked along the road past our porch. Men wore full Carhartt outfits, pointed at one another by way of greeting, and said things like "Wuh-oh, here comes trouble," or "How's your woman?" and discussed the routes they'd taken to get to the pole barn that served egg breakfasts. The word yes was universally pronounced *Yut*.

On break from mowing lawns a man actually told me I had a good job now, but once my looks went I'd have a hard time finding work that paid more than twelve dollars an hour.

My child occupied himself reading, learning guitar, and hanging out with two other misfit boys nicknamed C-Monkey and Baby Bear. They played basketball and explored abandoned buildings. The evening I found them putting one another into dryers at the laundromat I knew they'd hit the age where the town might break them.

No one really takes advice from people who got pregnant when they were teenagers and then went on to work mowing lawns. Even if that person had perfect standardized test scores, trained as a classical musician, and declined admission to an Ivy League school. I would go so far as to say *especially* if that person declined admission to an Ivy League school. So, I didn't have high hopes my child and his friends would listen to me.

Baby Bear was just starting to sweat when I opened the dryer door.

"Get in the Cessna," I told them. That's what we called the car because of the noise it made. "Do you guys want to end up mowing lawns for a living?"

"I don't think it would be that bad," said my musically inclined child, who had so far scored perfectly on standardized tests.

I slapped my forehead.

"There's a guy? At the end of this road? Who fishes for bats in the night with a fishing pole," Baby Bear said.

"Technically he fishes for them with insects," C-Monkey said.

"Uh yeah? That he puts on a hook? On a line? Connected to a pole?" Baby Bear said.

"Why is there gin in the glove compartment?" my child asked.

"In case of Negroni," I said.

"You should put the fishing-for-bats guy in your book," C-Monkey said.

My twelve-year-old child and his friends were the only people I knew who thought my book would be published.

I pulled over once we reached the Christmas lights; in the dark fall night, it was like looking into a sea of fireflies. A display of multicolored reindeer raised and lowered their necks as if they were grazing, or suddenly hearing the step of a hunter. The branches and trunks of trees were wrapped in an ethereal glow, like a ghostly electric forest that stretched back into the land.

They got out of the car and I took the liquor out of the glove compartment, then rummaged through garbage on the floor of the back seat for some empty take-out coffee cups.

"It's not going to be as good without the orange," my child said.

"Technically, Campari is made from the fruit of the myrtle-leaved orange tree," C-Monkey said. "So it won't be without orange."

"True," my child said, splashing a finger of the red spirit into our paper cups, following it with a capful of gin.

I raised my cup in the direction of the lights and the black water of the inlet beyond.

"It feels?" Baby Bear said, "like this is Christmas Eve."

Negroni (and variations)

LOVE 'EM OR HATE 'EM, Negronis are a classic hot-weather drink. Bitter, sweet, silky, bright . . . give it three sips the first time you try one, as Campari takes a little getting used to, to put it mildly.

Ingredients
1½ oz. London dry gin
¾ oz. Campari
¾ oz. Punt e Mes or comparable Italian sweet vermouth
2 dashes grapefruit bitters
2 dashes Angostura bitters
2 dashes rhubarb bitters
Orange peel or wedge, to garnish

How to Make It: Negronis are served in many ways; the essential thing is they be served very cold. As the Negroni is another vermouth drink, albeit one containing sweet Italian vermouth, don't shake it—stir with ice. So, either build the drink in a shaker, strain, and serve up with a twist, or alternately pour it over rocks with an orange wedge jammed in there (my personal favorite way to drink them).

You can even do what contributor to this volume Ms. Chambers does, and put all the above into a blender (sans garnish) with lots of ice and whiz it until it's a slushie, then drink it out of a highball with a straw.

The Negroni is a classic summer drink, but if you're anything like me, getting too drunk in the hot summer sun is no fun at all. (Spring and Fall are my personal Negroni seasons.) That said, if you like the taste of the Negroni, but also don't like passing out in a lawn chair after spoiling *Game of Thrones* for your friends (not that I'd know anything about that . . .) I'd suggest the Americano as a summer alternative. Skip the gin, and instead mix 1½ ounces of Campari and ¾ ounce Italian vermouth in a highball glass with the same bitters as above. Muddle with an orange wedge, fill glass with ice, and top it with seltzer.

Hey Bartender: Neat, But Not Straight Up!

. . . .

Some cocktails, you might just want to let a bartender mix for you. And is there a better setting for a short story than a bar?

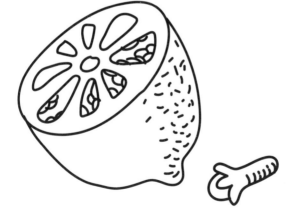

Vesper

THE VESPER COMES STRAIGHT FROM the pages of Ian Fleming's 1953 Bond novel *Casino Royale*. Bond considers a martini, then gives these instructions to the bartender instead: "Just a moment. Three measures of Gordon's, one of vodka, half a measure of Kina Lillet. Shake it very well until it's ice-cold, then add a large thin slice of lemon peel. Got it?"

Named for the Bond girl of *Casino Royale*, Vesper Lynd, the cocktail really is a revelation. It's boozy, vaguely lemony, with a faint herbal note from the combination of Lillet and gin. If you like martinis with a twist instead of an olive, the Vesper is something you ought to try.

You may have noticed that my proportions aren't the same as Fleming's. Well, there's a reason for that: Kina Lillet, now more commonly known as Lillet Blanc or Lillet Rouge, is an aperitif wine, vaguely similar to vermouth. The formula for Lillet changed in the 1980s, so older cocktail recipes are often in need of adjustment to get the balance right. (The last cocktail in this volume, the Corpse Reviver #2, also underwent such a change as I tinkered with the recipe.) I also prefer to stir the drink rather than shake it to make it less watery; that said, I do like the way water opens up the gin and the Lillet, so try it both ways and see what you like best. But if you try it both ways in the same night, make sure you're not driving anywhere after. The Vesper is a varsity-level cocktail.

Ingredients
2 oz. London dry gin
½ oz. vodka
¼ oz. Lillet Blanc
Lemon peel, to garnish

How to Make It: Pour everything save for the garnish into a shaker; stir with lots of cracked ice until cold and strain into a cocktail glass. Garnish with a lemon peel.

Take Flight

By Carrie Laben

I ASK THE WAITER FOR an Aviation and the guy in the lounge chair next to mine perks up, notices me noticing, and nods. I'd sized him up before I took the chair and he seems okay; about a decade older than me, solid, sunscreen smeared across his nose and his wedding ring still on.

"Good choice," he says.

"I always get one before I fly. Reminds the plane of what it's supposed to do."

"Heading home?"

"Heading on."

His phone beeps and he twists his lips apologetically. I shrug. He picks up, says "Hi hon," and I'm back to my own concerns, which are many and unpleasant. I could cancel. I just said I wouldn't, sort of, to this stranger, but I could.

The cocktail arrives quickly. It's a delicate almost-violet blue with a black cherry impaled on a pick. The little girl in me loves neon-red embalmed cherries just as much, and I've learned to live with the bartenders who make a sort of bastard gin sour and call it good, but it's always a pleasant surprise to find out that a place does things right.

People say this drink should be the color of the sky but the sky can be an array of different colors. The sky over Arenal Volcano, which I stare at as I take my first sip, is a more assertive blue than the cocktail, not quite the cliché of a robin's egg but maybe a darkish starling's egg. Who knows how the sky over Lake Junin looks right now. Could be the color of a bluebird, could be the color of a wolf. *Worrying won't change it*, I tell myself, but I know gin will ease my anxiety a lot faster than positive self-talk will. Another, deeper sip.

Eventually there's another beep as the man next to me ends his call. "Oh good, they made it right," he says when he turns back to look at my cocktail, which I've lowered by nearly half. "I'm not normally a snob, but my brother-in-law was one of the marketing guys who worked on bringing the purple stuff, the crème de violette, back from the dead. This one's about family pride."

"From the dead? They always made it in Europe, though, didn't they?"

"Close enough to dead." He laughs. "So where are you flying off to, if you don't mind me asking?"

Normally I might mind, but talking through this seems like a good idea and I'll never see this dude again. "Lake Junin. The Peruvian highlands."

"Peru? Why?"

"There's an endemic grebe . . ." He looks blank. "There's a couple of species of birds there that don't live anywhere else. One, this grebe, is pretty endangered. Might already be extinct." There, I said it out loud. It wasn't that I might die, though that seemed more real since Carl's plane went down. It was that I might die chasing after a bird that was itself dead. That seemed stupid.

"Ah, a bird-watcher. When you said Peru, I was worried you might be into weird stuff."

"What, weirder than going to a resort on top of a volcano?"

"It was my daughter's idea." He laughs again. "I promised her a trip for graduation, and I feel a lot safer having her sitting on a volcano with me than going to South Padre Island at spring break without me. You know what I mean?"

I know what he means, which is probably why I cried more about Carl than my actual dad. I steel my face and nod, sip. And I know that if I canceled my flight I could probably stay here and take him for a good few thousand bucks. I probably wouldn't even have to sleep with him—unlike the guy I catfished to fund this excursion. He's small potatoes but tempting enough to make this a working holiday. Plenty of birds in Costa Rica that I've yet to see, and that he could pay for.

"But isn't Peru a little . . . sketchy, anyway? They got those guerillas. Shining Path."

"Shining Path hasn't kidnapped any birders since 1990," I say more cheerfully than I feel. That was an ugly one, and everyone keeps bringing it up, jinxing my trip. "It's more the small planes that worry me. Small planes kill more great birders than anything. Dick Fitzner, Ted Parker, Carl . . ." This doesn't mean anything to him and I cut it off with another sip. I'm not going to do my private litany in front of someone else, not even a friendly stranger.

"Flying's safer than driving, though." After a moment he realizes how dumb and inapplicable that is all by himself, and adds, "I guess maybe not in Peru."

I could talk about how terrifying driving in the Andes is, too, but I'd rather not.

"They don't even have real airstrips, just a field of grass. And the route I'm flying they don't pressurize the cabins. The air masks drop when you get high enough and you breathe that way." And thank god someone thought to mention that one to me, or I might have died of a damn heart attack before the plane hit a single bump of turbulence. This is what birders, great ones, do, though. This is how you get to where the birds are.

I must look like I feel, because the guy doesn't laugh again, but frowns. "Well, maybe you shouldn't be doing that."

Hearing someone say that, especially now that there's some booze percolating in me, relights a very old spark. That was what I needed. I just didn't know it.

"If the grebe goes extinct, though . . ."

"Heck, it's just a bird. Besides, they'll probably be able to bring it back like they brought back the crème de violette; everyone said that was dead. They did a program about that on Nat Geo, they're gonna do the passenger pigeon and mammoths. Just like Jurassic Park." I can feel my heart lifting, my spine stiffening. "And your family . . . look, no offense, but you're young. You probably don't appreciate how upset people would be if something happened to you."

If one of the four guys I'm dating back in Chicago went through my stuff and found out about the other three I suppose that would, indeed, be upsetting for all of them. I suppress that smile behind another sip. More of a small gulp, actually.

His phone beeps again and he holds up a hand. "My daughter. I told her to check in every time she goes someplace new."

I give him a little *go on* gesture and as soon as he answers I drain my drink and stand. Steady. Perfect.

I leave without a good-bye. The shuttle to the airport leaves soon. And this guy, he doesn't even know what dead means.

Aviation

THE AVIATION IS ONE OF those hotly contested recipes that everyone has an opinion about. Should it be purple due to a generous measure of crème de violette? (No.) Or is a more modest dribble of the liqueur, turning it the palest of pale gray-blues the right way to mix it? (Yes!) Or, should you skip the flowery liqueur entirely, and use more maraschino liqueur? (Of course you should not.)

I say this, but I'm also a big fan of mixing drinks to your own taste, so do whatever you want. But, if you want to know my thoughts on the matter, and presumably you do as you bought this book (or are at least perusing it in the bookstore), here's my take: the Aviation is a great gin cocktail to have under your belt, and one all about balance. It should accentuate the flavor of your gin, framing the botanicals with lemon and flower tastes, not masking them with overpowering sourness or sweetness. This is my proven and true way of making the drink; others would recoil at the additional sweetener, or reduction in the typical amount of lemon. Play around with it!

Ingredients

2 oz. London dry gin

½ oz. lemon juice

½ oz. maraschino liqueur

1 tsp. crème de violette

1 tsp. simple syrup or agave nectar

Maraschino cherry or lemon twist, to garnish

How to Make It: Put all ingredients save the garnish in a cocktail shaker with lots of ice and combine. Strain it into a chilled cocktail glass or coupe; garnish with either a real maraschino cherry or a lemon twist.

Maraschino is a word Americans usually associate with cherries—those bleached and dyed treats we put atop sundaes and stick in sub-par cocktails. Yeah, I said it.

You can get real maraschino cherries these days—indeed, please do; any drinks in this book that call for a cherry garnish deserve a real brandied cherry, as do you my friend—but maraschino liqueur is something else entirely. There are a few brands out there; Luxardo is the most common. Basically, maraschino liqueur is made from marasca (sour) cherries, distilled to make it clear. It's not all that sweet, but it does enhance drinks with subtle sweetness and notes of fruit. Many pre-Prohibition cocktails call for it, and usually just a bit of it, so it's worth investing in. Even if you're making cocktails regularly and in earnest, a bottle will last you years. Invest!

Marmot Season

By Jeff VanderMeer

W HEN I GOT TO THE island, I discovered nothing I had asked for was in my pack. Instead, there was a thermos containing Moscow Mules and one trademark copper cup. This was clearly an "F-U" about my research from the U of Central-South Michigan and certain parties thereof. Certainly, it could not be an "F-U" from the locals who had prepared my pack because none of them knew I was a drinker; I had been careful to tipple in secret. Mark and Cindy, the joint Biology chairs, knew that I drank Moscow Mules, although if you were to ask around you would discover that I did not drink them to the profusion that some on the faculty claimed. Certainly, I was the only one in the Biological Sciences Department coherent enough to point out all the terrible inefficiencies. "We're not living in the 1990s." "MC," as I'd dubbed them, did not appreciate being reminded they had decided to stay stuck in the Stone Age. But someone had to do it, for the good of the others.

By the time I discovered I had no food or water or any of my intricate scientific equipment, my boat driver had already left for the mainland and I was alone on a temperate mountainous island populated by wolves and wild cattle and something I encountered at various points along the trail, something that hissed suggestively from the bushes but would never allow itself to be seen. As MC and my boat driver knew, I had an aversion to bodies of water and also to moving my arms to stay afloat—thus my decision to climb a mountain on an island to examine the rare marmot *Marmota sparticanicus minor* was an act of conspicuous bravery that I had tried to advertise to MC and the rest of the Biology faculty so that they would understand how committed I was to the department.

My boat driver was due to return in three days, as it would take a day to make it to the top of the mountain and a day to complete my initial research goals, and then a day to make it back down again. But perhaps, I thought, MC had interfered with this schedule as well, as I remembered being puzzled as the boat driver had shouted "See you in two weeks!" and had waved back smiling, believing that utterance to be some kind of brutal local joke. Either way, sitting on my duff at the rotted pier would help no one. *Surely*, I thought, *I can live off the land for a short period of time. Find roots and find berries and perhaps lick the water off the stems of succulents.*

It should be noted that the entire time I was performing these clumsy mental gymnastics the thermos of Moscow Mules seemed to gleam and perhaps even glow in the bronzing midday light, and the clank of the glass against the thermos in the pack made me as thirsty as if I'd been dropped in the middle of a desert to wither, desiccate, and husk. But I soldiered on, as they say, and began to make my way up the mountain. Past an abandoned town graffitied by its departing youth—a combination of the normal tags and a sad profusion of bad comic-book like depictions of *M. sparticanicus minor* giving the onlooker the bird. Oddly, perhaps, this presighting cheered me up, bolstered by having taken a swig from the thermos. The people here, now long gone, had known good old MSM and incorporated it into the local iconography. Good.

Not so good when, an hour later, I came across the *same* derelict town once again. After an initial moment of horror and creepiness I realized that, no, I was not in a bad horror movie, but had instead missed the trailhead and circled back around without realizing. For a moment, it had crossed my mind that perhaps some force more malevolent than merely MC and an ungrateful University of Central-South Michigan had switched out my pack. But this was clearly residue from my hobby of watching too many indie horror flicks on those rare, yet not unusual, nights when I stayed home rather than partake of the local culture of bars and taverns.

Having corrected my course, I quickly scarpered after giving the actually excellent Moscow Mules their due by pouring out a mere trace into the cup. They were just as good as water, in my opinion—better, in fact, given the murk-quality I observed during the ascent. Anyway, having corrected my course, I quickly scampered up the side of the mountain, through the old-growth firs and pines, doing my best to think like *M. sparticanicus minor* in the way I scurried and, to be candid, nibbled on that local vegetation that looked edible.

By the time I reached a ravine of cracked and broken cedar logs, overgrown with lichen and ferns, I had become both enough of a *M. sparticanicus minor* and enough of a drunk that, lithe and marmot like and with any number of bruises and cuts I didn't feel, I made my way up that hell-field like some land-bound human salmon leaping upstream in an ecstasy of giving "F-U's" back to MC and my university. I would make it. I would ascend and descend and by god I would use the Moscow Mules as fuel.

By the late afternoon, having seen the shadows of either shadows or wolves interwoven with the lush landscape, I approached the summit, and the monk's tonsure of forest and clearing that MSM favored. "High-altitude, high-functioning marmots," as I had always described them.

By late afternoon the thermos was empty, supplemented by stream water I unfortunately did not realize until too late was fortified with frog spawn, and I had taken to warning off the local wildlife by banging the cup against any random tree that didn't frighten me with bark-face. My legs were indeed rubbery and my thoughts had grown maudlin, remembering my brief affair with Cindy several years back, and how even now it was clear she had not left the M in MC because of her commitment to running the Biological Sciences Department, and how although she had told me the kid was M's, not mine, perhaps if I had not been so fiercely attentive to the needs of *M. sparticanicus minor* things might have gone differently, no matter what the kid's origins.

At which point, near that halo'd summit, MSM appeared before me! Doubled! Tripled! Such that I banged my cup in triumph like a beggar suddenly gifted with a stream of gold coins falling from on high.

"You are such a cuteness and a lifting of spirits," I faux-scolded the marmots, which resolved into a single individual in a most curious way.

"You've blown your whole life," MSM responded, or I believe it responded, for they have not since spoken to me. "I have no need of your ministrations or your taxonomy." And then disappeared into the underbrush, with me stumbling after, shouting, "Come back, MSM! Don't you know me, MSM! Don't you know of me?"

That was almost six months ago. No boat ever came again to this remote location, nor may ever come. But I am holding my own. I have since become quite assimilated into the MSM community, and I have thrived in the picking of berries and the finding of nuts, and if every once in a while an MSM individual disappears, I cannot be held responsible as a healthy cull is good for animal populations.

But I do wish—oh how I wish—for the healing libation of a good Moscow Mule, or at least some sort of beverage free of frog spawn.

Moscow Mule

THE MOSCOW MULE WENT FROM relative obscurity to having a place on every decent bar's menu practically overnight, it seems. And with good reason! They are delicious, easily prepared, hard to screw up, and please a lot of palates—even those accustomed to nothing more adventurous than a gin and ginger ale. Or just ginger ale. They also almost universally delight the uninitiated the first time when they're served properly, in a copper mug. (Haters will say it makes no difference to the finished beverage; I usually reply by citing the aesthetic difference between drinking a cola out of a plastic bottle versus a can.)

Ingredients
1½ oz. vodka
Ice
Ginger beer
Lime wedge, to garnish

How to Make It: Measure 1½ ounces of vodka into a copper mug, add ice, and top with ginger beer—the good stuff. There are lots of good brands these days; take advantage of them! Squeeze in a lime wedge and stir. Serve. Enjoy as you observe the marmots.

Ugh, garnishes.

I say *ugh* here because garnishes are rarely done well. Why stick a lime or lemon wedge or wheel on the edge of a glass? Is it supposed to be a prank, or perhaps a trap meant for enemies, the purpose of which is to get citrus juice in someone's nose or eye? Why use American maraschino cherries at all, when they do nothing but make a drink look like it's meant for children? Why stick an entire chicken wing in a Bloody Mary?

The answers to these questions are, respectively, "incompetence," "cheapness," and "late-capitalist society's desire for excess that seeks to distract us from the meaninglessness of our existence." But don't worry; I am here to guide you back to the light.

Garnishes should serve a purpose. A burst of salt from an olive enhances one's experience of a martini. A real brandied cherry gives a bitter drink a bit of lusciousness and sweetness. Citrus peels add their natural oils to drinks, adding aroma and a bit of mouthfeel. So, garnish wisely, and with a purpose in mind. If you think a slice of candied ginger will add a bit of fancy sparkle to a Mule or another gingery drink, give it a whirl. But if you or your guest finds it boops you in the nose every time you take a sip, that's experience teaching you a lesson.

In the Sky She Floats

by Gina Marie Guadagnino

ERSPIRATION PRICKING AT HER NECK, her back stuck unpleasantly to the horsehair sofa, and, head pounding, Lennie abruptly gave up any further attempt to sleep. The room, which had been brightly lit and packed with sweating, Charlestoning bodies when she had dozed off, was now dark and empty, save for a man in a white dinner jacket who lay draped crossways over a wingbacked chair snoring placidly.

Lennie lifted the beaded train of her skirt, then picked her way across the room to the window, shoes in her other hand, tiptoeing on stockinged feet around the discarded bottles that littered the floor. She eased the casement open wider and slipped out into the humid predawn air on the fire escape.

The sky was still dark, but the lights of Manhattan spread out before her in a twinkling grid. From this vantage point, Lennie could look down and see the motorcars crawling along the avenues like glittering insects, the streetlights glinting off their polished shells of steel and chrome. Off to her left, the black swell of the East River, where the inky sky was just beginning to fade to pale blue over Brooklyn. She leaned on the railing of the fire escape, curling her toes around the cool metal, angling her face upward toward the warm wind that swept up the avenue.

"Well, ain't you a picture, sweetheart?" a girl's voice said.

Lennie started, dropping one of her shoes. She watched as it tumbled to the sidewalk eight stories below, then turned to the window to face the interloper. The girl, about her own age, sat on the windowsill, her evening gown rucked up around her knees. Her wide eyes sparkled.

Lennie put her free hand on her hip and glared at the girl. "You owe me a shoe!" She held the pose for all of five seconds before they both dissolved into laughter, and Lennie flung the other heel over the railing for good measure.

"Pax," the girl said, holding her hands up. "Hang on a tic, I've got just the remedy." She disappeared back inside the apartment, and Lennie sat down on the edge of the fire escape, hiking up her skirt and letting her legs dangle over the street below. A few moments later, the girl reappeared, a cocktail glass filled with ruddy liquid in each hand. She handed one to Lennie and sat silently beside her. They clinked the rims, saluting each other.

Lennie sipped. The drink was strong, just a little sweet, and cold. At first it was harsh, but gradually, the liquor mellowed on her palate. A single cherry glowered like a hazy sunrise at the bottom of the glass.

The sky was growing lighter, a warm blue light tinting the sky over Brooklyn. Already the sound of the El and the motorcars was rising. An anemic breeze wafted off the river, bringing with it the brackish smell of oyster shells. Lennie could feel the thin silk of her dress clinging to her body in the humidity, damp beneath her arms and the swell of her breasts. Beads of condensation pooled against the side of the glass. She ran her tongue along the rim, and sensed that the girl was looking at her. She raised the glass.

"Say, what's in this drink anyhow?" she asked.

The girl leaned back on her hands, looking up at the disappearing crescent moon. "It's called a Manhattan."

"Like the island?"

"Like the island."

Lennie took another sip. "It's good."

"Like the island," the girl repeated. She smiled crookedly and stuck out her hand in a jaunty, gentlemanly fashion. "They call me Maisie. What do you go by, sweetheart?"

"I'm Lennie," she replied, shaking hands. "Pleased to make your acquaintance."

Maisie shrugged, a small smile still playing at the corners of her mouth. "Everyone who tastes one of my cocktails says that."

"It's awful good." Lennie took another sip. "What's in it?"

Maisie said nothing for a moment. The pale pink light that was growing over Brooklyn gave warmth to her pallor. She sipped her drink. Then she said, "Do you know why they call it a Manhattan? You'll never guess."

Lennie cocked her head. "Then why don't you tell me?"

Maisie took a meditative sip of her beverage. "Where're you from, sweetheart?"

Lennie took her time answering, sliding up her skirt to unpin her stockings from her garters and roll them off her legs. "Baxter Street," she said finally.

Maisie rolled her eyes. "You know that's not what I mean."

"I was born and raised there," Lennie said, smoothing the silk out on her lap.

"You might have been born there, but your ancestors came from a lot further away. Me, now, I'm half-Irish, half-Swede, which accounts for me being so fair." Maisie regarded her, narrowing her blue eyes. "So, let me guess. Hair that dark," she said, reaching over to tuck a stray curl behind Lennie's ear. "All those pretty curls, aquiline nose, eyes so full I could drown in 'em. Greek?"

"Other side of the Mediterranean, I'm afraid. Italian."

"Oh? I took you for the tenth Muse."

"Well, think of me as Venus instead," Lennie said, smiling. "With boughs of myrtle in my hand."

"Rising up on the clam shell? Oh, you'd be a sight! My point," said Maisie, taking another sip of her cocktail, "is that this city was built by people who came from somewhere else. We're all of us immigrants, once you scratch the surface."

"That may be, cara mia," said Lennie. "And every now and then I might slip into the mother tongue. But I guess I always think of myself as an American."

"Of course you are, Miss Baxter Street," Maisie said comfortably. "Same as me. Same as the rest of the poor slobs sleeping it off in there. But we're all of us immigrants, at the end of the day. Italian, Irish, German, Chinese. None of the best things in this town are *really* from here anyway. They're a mix that people brought from all over the world, and cobbled together here to make something new and different. Which brings me," she said, raising her glass to Lennie, "back to this cocktail."

"Which you seem to be taking your time telling me about," Lennie said with a laugh.

"Good things come, as the saying goes. You start with rye. That's Canadian whiskey. They make it after the Irish style, blended, you know. I know a fella who drives in over the border when Lake Erie freezes. Then you add vermouth—nothing like good French vermouth, chérie—and see you stir it well. Now, there's some as say you can do a bit of orange peel for the garnish, but for my money, you had better have a real maraschino cherry, with a dash of the liquor. And then, and here's the trick, you stir it all together with ice until it's so well blended that you can't tell the Irish part from the Canadian part from the French part from the Italian part. And when it's all mixed together into something that could never be from any other part of the world except New York, that's when you can call it a Manhattan, sweetheart. Because that's the story of all of us. We're all from someplace else."

She finished the remainder of her cocktail and rested her head on Lennie's shoulder, her short cropped blonde bob brushing Lennie's cheek. Gazing out into the predawn light, she murmured, "The silver moon is set. The Pleiades are gone."

"Hmm. Maybe *you're* the muse around here," Lennie said, smoothing Maisie's blonde hair back from where it tickled at her chin.

"I most certainly could be, sweetheart," Maisie said, popping the cherry from her empty glass into her mouth. "On a morning like this, I feel like I could be anything."

Lennie sipped the rest of her drink slowly, watching as the ruby liquid dwindled in her glass, as the pink sky began to bleed to red at the horizon line. When the sun broke over the Brooklyn skyline, Lennie's lips found Maisie's. They tasted of whiskey, of cherries, of Manhattan.

Manhattan

It's true that in general I have strong opinions about cocktails, and my opinion about the Manhattan is very strong indeed. Unlike many, I don't especially care whether it's based around bourbon or rye—both are great, and while the spiciness of rye makes for a complicated and delicious cocktail, my Wild Turkey 101 Manhattans are not to be flexed with. And yet I cannot abide a "perfect" Manhattan: one made with both sweet and dry vermouth. I think they're filthy and wrong. Sweet vermouth is the only acceptable vermouth for a Manhattan. Also: bitters. Sure, you can get fancy, and use cherry bitters, or bourbon barrel bitters, or whatever . . . but Angostura is really what goes best in a Manhattan. Sometimes, there's a reason for tradition. Also, I included the lemon peel garnish as a concession to history, but really, go for the cherry. Sure, the lemony notes are nice, but the squidgy lusciousness of a real brandied cherry is to me the only garnish for this drink.

People will come at me about the dash of soda water but I really think it makes the drink. Leave it out if you're a purist; include it if you'd like to open up the botanicals in your vermouth and add a bit of mouthfeel to the drink.

Ingredients

2 oz. bourbon or rye
1 oz. sweet Italian vermouth
Several dashes Angostura bitters
Cherry or lemon peel, to garnish
Soda water

How to Make It: Pour everything save for the garnish and the soda water into a shaker, then stir with lots of cracked ice until very cold. Do not shake! This isn't a matter of opinion, like a martini or Vesper. It's just bad form to shake a Manhattan; neither the color nor the texture will be right if you do. Anyway, strain into a chilled coupe; top with maybe just a tablespoon of soda water and garnish with a cherry. Enjoy with a friend.

Old Fashioned

THE OLD FASHIONED IS A drink with a reputation marred by bad bartending and a fundamental misunderstanding of the beverage. It should not be a fruity, fizzy thing; it is a serious bourbon cocktail, and it should be treated as such. Its simple ingredients ought to frame the natural flavors of the spirit, not mask them. Thankfully, craft bartenders are doing God's work, bringing the Old Fashioned back to its former glory in bars all across America, using great small batch bourbons and local bitters. You can recreate the glory easily at home, however—the Old Fashioned is not a difficult drink to make. You just have to use quality ingredients, and not go crazy with muddling oranges and goofing the drink up with cherries.

Ingredients
Sugar cube
Bitters
Soda water
2 oz. bourbon
Orange peel, to garnish

How to Make It: In a cocktail shaker, add a sugar cube and saturate it with Angostura bitters, or a mix of Angostura and fancier bitters. Try orange, cherry, or bourbon barrel, for a change. Splash in a bit of soda water—a tablespoon or two, no more—and muddle until the cube and bitters are dissolved. Pour in the bourbon, stir, and add a few cubes of ice and shake. Pour over ice cubes in an Old Fashioned glass, and garnish with a thick slice of orange peel, twisting it to get the orange oil over the surface and running the peel around the edge of the glass before dunking it in.

Around the World in a Daze: Drinking Everywhere

It's a great big world out there, and thankfully it is full of liquor. Our authors are going to circumnavigate the globe, from England to . . . Oakland?

A Hot Night
at Hinky Dinks

. . . .

By Will Viharo

OAKLAND, CALIFORNIA, 1944
A warm offshore breeze wafted in from San Pablo Avenue through the open double doors, putting all the bar patrons in a tropical mood despite the arid atmosphere, but also giving some of the more restless drinkers the jitters. Californians call it earthquake weather. Anything could happen, at any moment. A bloodred sunset drenched the Bay in ominous hues. "Caravan" by Duke Ellington played obliviously on the jukebox as if everything would be all right.

Hinky Dinks proprietor and chief bartender Vic Bergeron turned around, reached up, and took down a bottle of J. Wray Nephew rum from the bamboo shelf behind him, which complemented the other-wise rustic décor.

"This is seventeen years old, from Jamaica," he said to his two friends, Ham and Carrie Guild, who were visiting all the way from Tahiti. They both nodded, pleased, as Vic poured two ounces of the premium aged rum into a silver shaker filled with crushed ice, and followed it with two ounces of Red Heart Jamaican Rum, for the sake of a sublime, though subtle, complexity. He then added the tart juice from two freshly squeezed limes, an ounce of orange curacao from Holland, half an ounce of Rock Candy Syrup, an ounce of French Orgeat, shook it up well, then poured the combined ingredients into two chilled glasses, also already filled with crushed ice, waiting on the bar. "Just a little something new I've been experimenting with," Vic said with pride.

Ham and Carrie sipped their cocktails tentatively at first, but once the rich, tangy concoction made their taste buds tingle and their brain cells swoon, they enthusiastically expressed their approval.

"This is delicious," Ham said. "It tastes like the islands!"

"Wait!" Vic said suddenly. "I forgot something. Don't take another sip yet." He reached below the bar, pulled out some sprigs of fresh mint, and garnished both drinks. It was the perfect final touch on his masterpiece.

With another sip, Carrie declared, "Maita'I Roa Ae!"

"What?" said Vic with a bemused grin.

"It means 'very good' in Tahitian," Carrie explained. "Out of this world!"

"Then that's what I'll call it!" Vic said. "Mai tai! I just hope nobody tries to steal the formula. I have a feeling it will be my liquid legacy. Keep it to yourselves for now."

Vic mixed himself a newly christened Mai Tai with the same recipe cut in half, since he couldn't afford to get loaded on the job, and this was strong stuff, as both nature and his experimentation had intended. The three chitchatted as they enjoyed Vic's triumphant creation.

Artie Shaw's version of "Temptation" was playing when a beautiful, voluptuously composed young woman of ambiguous ethnic origin, dressed in a very tight, low-cut flower patterned gown and black high-heeled pumps, strode in and sat down beside Ham and Carrie.

Vic was immediately entranced, as was Ham. Carrie bristled. The stranger's intense sexual allure was both intoxicating and intimidating. No one noticed that the temperature of the bar had suddenly dropped as a rogue fog bank defied the high-pressure system dominating the region, infusing Hinky Dinks with a light, cool mist, her long, black, wavy locks glistening with mystical dewdrops.

"What'll it be, miss?" Vic said, shivering slightly.

"I'll have what they're having," she said, her voice husky and seductive.

"It's not for sale," Carrie snapped. "This is a private party, lady."

"Coming right up," Vic said as he began preparing another Mai Tai.

Carrie glared at the strange woman, and noticed that the pupils of her eyes were a deep scarlet.

When her drink was set before the woman, she didn't even take a sip. Instead she asked, "What's in it?"

Entranced, Vic told her the exact ingredients and their precise measurements. Carrie gasped. Ham just polished off his Mai Tai, and casually requested another. Vic complied.

"Aren't you at least going to drink it?" Carrie asked the stranger.

"I never drink . . . rum," she said.

"Then why did you ask for a cocktail?" Carrie said.

"Because I'm thirsty, but not for alcohol."

The woman then got up from her seat, walked behind the bar, slipped her gown down, and kicked it off her shapely gams, exposing her large, firm, breasts and impeccably coiffed genitalia. She was now standing in front of Vic in all her natural glory, wearing nothing but those shiny black pumps. Vic was paralyzed, slightly rocking on his wooden leg, as she embraced him, kissed him, and then opened her luscious crimson lips wide to sink her fangs into his throat.

"Vic!" Carrie shouted, snapping him out of his daze. Reflexively Ham—as spontaneously heroic as his namesake in the Doc Savage pulp novels he loved so much—grabbed a tiki statue off the bar, broke off the corner of its wooden head on the edge of the counter, and handed it to Vic. He impaled the woman in her well-endowed chest with the jagged edge. Blood spurted down the curves of her torso and rounded hips and all over Vic's authentic Hawaiian aloha shirt.

The entire bar broke into spontaneous applause. But then a burst of staccato machine gunfire immediately spoiled the celebration as five large men wearing dark pinstripe suits with brightly-colored ties barged in, shooting up the jukebox as well as several valuable bottles of rum and a few tiki mugs lining the shelves behind the bar. Vic ducked for cover as Hinky Dinks filled with screams.

A man dressed in an expertly pressed white suit with an open blue shirt and a straw cabana hat walked in casually behind the armed intruders. Vic peered over the edge of the bar and recognized him as Ernest Raymond Beaumont Gantt, better known these days as Donn Beach, owner of the most successful Polynesian restaurant in Hollywood, Don the Beachcomber.

"I see you've met Lorelei," Donn said dryly to Vic, peering over the bar at the curvaceous corpse, the shard of the tiki statue still in her chest, blood bubbling from the wound like it was an enflamed scorpion bowl.

"You know her?" Vic said.

"I met her while on vacation in Bermuda, and brought her back home with me," Donn explained. "Even though she hates the sun and never goes outside in the daytime. She shared some native recipes with me. Including a little something I call . . . the Mai Tai."

"I don't believe it," Vic said. "Next thing you know, Harry Owen will be mixing pineapple juice with cheap rum and grenadine, garnished with a cherry, and calling it a Mai Tai!"

"It's my drink, Vic," Donn said. "Well, actually it was Lorelei's, but she's no longer with us, thanks to you. I first served it ten years ago at my joint down south. It's somewhat different than yours—you know, better. And it was *first*. So just forget you ever mixed that cocktail, Vic, and my boys here won't have to cruise back some evening and help you close up shop—for good."

"You'll never get away with this!" Vic said. "Oakland is now the home of the Mai Tai—not just the drive-by!"

"Too late, Vic. Sorry."

"How did you even know about this?" Vic asked, exasperated. "I just started playing around with it last week!"

"Lorelei was my most resourceful spy," he said. "I could never understand her ways, but she always got the job done . . . until now. You're a murderer, Vic. No more Mai Tais for you behind bars. Maybe you can request one for your last meal on Death Row, though."

But then Lorelei's pin-up figure suddenly melted into an oozing pile of gore and mysterious smoke, rendering her body unidentifiable . . . and unrecognizable as human remains. The cool mist engulfing the bar evaporated, and everyone was perspiring once again, and from more than just the heat.

"Damn, I didn't see that coming." Donn grimaced. "I guess you're off the hook, Vic. How did you even know she was a—"

"I get around, too, you know," Vic said. "I know her kind. And yours."

"Listen, why don't we just all have a round of Mai Tais and talk about this," Donn said. "Maybe we can share the recipe?"

"It died with her," Vic said, "and you're not getting it from me."

"Well, can I at least try it?"

Vic looked back at the shelf and the rows of broken bottles, rum dripping down and mixing with the gruesome bodily fluids that had once been Lorelei.

"I guess I got enough for a few more rounds," Vic said. "Have a seat."

Donn and his mob of gun-toting goons occupied the bamboo chairs around those of Ham and Carrie, still sitting on the floor in a state of shock, wondering how they ever got mixed up with a peglegged character like Vic in the first place.

Soon everyone was drunk and friendly. Donn promised to back off his threat, deciding there was room in the world for more than one Mai Tai recipe.

"Even though mine is the best, if not the original," Vic insisted.

"History will be the judge of that," Donn said with a shrug, downing his fourth Mai Tai. Donn had heaped enough dough on the counter for everyone in the bar to sample a Mai Tai, excluding one loner that declined. In a very dark corner of the bar, a werewolf was drinking a Pina Colada.

His hair was perfect.

"Sorry I missed up your place," Donn said to Vic in a happy slur. "Violence is not normally my way of doing business."

Vic smiled and said, "Forget it, Donn. It's Oaktown."

Mai Tai

(Serves Two)

A N ICONIC TIKI DRINK OPENS our "Around the World" section. Yes, it is a far cry from the totally delicious Trader Vic's recipe most people (and vampires) turn to when they want a Mai Tai, but there's a reason for that—*this* recipe was reverse-engineered from the amazing Mai Tai they serve in the Li Po Lounge in San Francisco, California. I once drank two in a single evening, against the advice of the bartender, and while it's difficult to say if that was the drunkest I've ever been in my life, my life choices that night certainly produced one of the worst hangovers I've ever experienced. So, consume with care, because these are delicious and powerful.

The sign at the Li Po Lounge called for Whaler's dark rum and Castillo silver rum. Neither are too expensive to invest in, but if you have a silver and a dark rum on hand, go for those. The 151 adds power to the mix, and the grenadine a pleasant pomegranate note to the fruity Mai Tai mix. (Yes, mix! I know I'm usually not all about them, but that's what they use at the Li Po Lounge, and anyway, it's easier than buying a bunch of juices and compounding them. Tiki drinks are all about relaxation, after all.)

So, what's up with the Chinese Whiskey? I list it as optional because while it's used in the original, and gives the drink a floral note that makes it even more heady and tropical and delightful and sensory, it's damn near impossible to find. What they use at the Li Po Lounge is "Mui Kwe Lu," imported by the Wing Lee Wai wine merchants. It's a type of baiju, or distilled liquor, made from sorghum and roses. As far as I can tell, it's close to impossible to procure, though they do sell little bottles of it as a souvenir at the actual bar. That's pretty impractical for the vast majority of our readers, however, so just leave it out—or substitute a teensy dash of rosewater if you happen to have a bottle lying about. And yes, you can find rose-scented sorghum baiju in many Chinese supermarkets, but usually it's salty cooking wine, or just plain wrong in some other way. I did a lot of searching before a friend procured a bottle for me during a trip to San Francisco.

Ingredients
2 oz. dark rum
2 oz. silver rum
1 oz. Bacardi 151
½ oz. grenadine
4 oz. Mai Tai mix (yep, I said it)
1½ oz. Chinese whiskey (optional)
Ice

How to Make It: Dump everything in a blender and blend it up with 2–3 cups of ice until nice and smooth. Drink slowly out of some sort of ridiculous vessel, like a coconut or tiki mug, through a straw preferably, and garnish with whatever you like. It's a tiki drink. Put a tiny umbrella in there, a pineapple wedge improbably paired with a maraschino cherry; go nuts. To be fair, though, the original had no garnish, and was served to me in an old plastic cup, and was just fine like that.

Shochu

No RECIPE HERE, JUST SOME preparation notes, thoughts, and feelings.

I traveled to Japan a few years ago, and while I had some good cocktails there, especially in Tokyo, what really stood out to me was shochu.

Unlike sake, which is a brewed, rice-based wine, shochu is a distilled beverage that can be made of various starches. Perhaps it's that I don't care for sake, and as such don't typically explore liquor menus at Japanese restaurants, but I'd never heard of shochu before my trip to Japan. I'm happy to say I found it to be a tasty and versatile distillate, whether it's served neat, on the rocks, with hot water (mizuwari), or mixed with other alcohol.

Unlike the more floral, more fruity sake, shochu is crisp, flavorful, and dry. Though some varieties get up to 45% ABV, most come in around 25%—and it pairs really well with food, meaning you can sip on it all afternoon at your favorite izakaya as you sit with your friends eating delicious snacks. You can also buy shochu at any convenience store, in a bottle or a box. Indeed, one of my fondest memories of my trip is of hanging out with a friend in a hotel room in Nara, eating a onigiri procured from a 7–11 and drinking shochu from the same, watching a show where a Japanese man in a fedora and trench coat "investigated" why everyone around the world loves donburi (rice with meat) so much. "You ate the evidence, senpai!" his lovely assistant cried, toward the end.

Soju, the Korean version of shochu, is fairly popular these days. Jinro brand soju can be found in just about any liquor store, but Japanese shochu remains a specialty item. But, it's worth it to hunt some down. If you find a liquor store that stocks it, snap up a bottle and try it. My favorite way is on the rocks; I think cold brings out the lovely notes of whatever it's been distilled from, be it buckwheat (soba), barley (*mugi*), sweet potato (*imo*), or rice (*kome*). Then again, on a cold night, shochu with hot water is relaxing, delicious, and warming.

One More Night to Be Pirates

by Libby Cudmore

WE USED TO PRETEND WE were pirates. The back deck was our ship as we sailed across long summer days toward desert islands under the maple tree. Some afternoons, Armand's dad would bring us ginger beer in tall glasses with ice. *Like real pirates drank*, he told us.

As teenagers, we realized we could add rum to it. The deck was no longer a pirate ship, but was still our refuge; we'd sneak through fences and cut across yards after curfew to sit with our backs to the brick, cold glasses in hand, warm spice on our tongues. One night we got the idea to bury a treasure box and dig it up ten years later. We assembled only the most important things—a mix CD, a photo his mother took of us at Niagara Falls, the spoils of battles fought, sealed with blood pricked from our fingers. That was back when we thought our anchors would always hold, that our ships wouldn't drift in the night. I still have the scar on my index finger. I still taste his kiss whenever ginger passes my lips.

* * *

"Are you sure this is the right house?" I asked as he pulled the car up across from a blue clapboard house at the top of the Warwick Street cul-de-sac. "It looks completely different." The front porch was gone, and most of the small yard had been paved over for a patio set. I knew his family had sold it to some new-money trash after they moved back to New Hampshire, but I didn't expect the new owners to destroy it.

"I think I'd remember the house I spent the majority of my life in, Morgan," Armand said. "Christ, what kind of asshole paves over their front lawn? You should have seen the SUV they left in. You could fit a soccer team in there."

Now what we had to do was more important than ever. "You've checked the lights? The alarm?"

He nodded. "Last night I did a test run," he said. "The Andersons' old house is for sale, so no one's there. Mr. Braun still lives on the other side, and totally deaf now. His wife died a few years ago. My parents sent flowers. But he's got a live-in nurse; she sneaks outside for a smoke every so often."

"What do we do if she comes out?" I said.

"Hide," he said. "When we get to the backyard, you'll see that the tree has been taken down and replaced with a playset." He grinned. "A pirate ship playset. We should be able to duck in there."

"They didn't have to tear down the tree for that," I grumbled. "They could have put it anywhere else in the yard."

"Not if they were going to have the above-ground pool," he said.

"For fuck's sake."

He patted my hand. "Cheer up, matey," he said. "The back porch is still standing."

That brought out a little smile. "Aye aye."

* * *

The backyard might as well have been Disneyland for all the garbage crammed into it. The pool, the pirate ship, a hideous picnic bench with umbrella, a propane grill so pristine I doubt it had ever been used. All the trappings of an empty suburban life. I kicked a beach ball and it bounced, half-deflated, off the porch. "How are we even going to find it?" I asked. "All this crap is disorienting me."

Armand stood still for a second, walking over every inch of his memory, hands clasped to his mouth as though in prayer. "There," he said, pointing to the pirate ship. "Underneath."

Through the glass door of the back porch I could see the old oak bar that took up the corner of the living room. Glad to see that they had left some pieces standing. I tested the sliding door. To my surprise, it gave. We looked at each other, a silent dare. I took the first step.

We closed the door quietly behind us. The room was partially illuminated by streetlights, but even if the sun were up, we wouldn't have recognized the space. The bar was all that remained of the past. It wasn't even about new couches and paint and appliances. It was the smell. The aura. The grandfather clock was in his parents' condo but the *tick tick tick* of passing time was louder than ever.

He wandered the halls. I ducked behind the bar and pulled out a bottle of rum. In the minifridge I found ginger beer. At least these people did something right. I got ice from the freezer and had two drinks ready by the time he got back. I handed him a glass, already wet with condensation. "Like pirates used to drink," I said.

* * *

The pirate ship playhouse was hollow underneath, the air stale with the odor of hot plastic. We barely fit in the space; me with the flashlight, him with a trowel taken from the garage.

"You ever bring Tessa here?" I asked, setting down the flashlight to take a drink.

"Nah," Armand said. "She wouldn't get anything out of it. 'Hey, let's drive four hours to look at a house I lived in half a decade before we met.' Besides." He paused to take a drink, wiping the glass across his flushed forehead. "It just never felt right. This was our space. Sacred, almost."

After Will handed me the divorce papers and before my mom moved to Modesto, I used to drive five hours home on weekends, cry in my old bed, and sit in her borrowed car outside this house. He was never there, newly married to Tessa and settled in Boston, but it was a bittersweet reminder of a time when things made sense.

"I hit something," he said. He set down the trowel and wiped away the dirt with his hands. A wooden box with a rusting hinge, the one he made in shop class, stained to look like cherry, still intact. "Should we open it here?"

My heart beat a little faster. "I can't wait a minute longer."

It was all there. The photo, the two of us smiling in front of Niagara Falls. A notebook-sized Jolly Roger I won for him at the fair. A mix CD of Tragically Hip songs his cousin Doug made during a family reunion in Toronto, where we stayed up by a dying fire pit and he explained poetry through clouds of menthol smokes lifted from the pack his dad left on the picnic table.

But our biggest prize was Jeremy Van Owen's nylon wallet, with the thick chain and the laminated naked picture of Jeri Ryan. Armand had stolen out of his gym locker in retaliation for the prank he and my then-friend Kaitlin Olson played on me where he pretended he was in love with me, asked me to the movies and then cackled in the bushes with her as I stood forlornly outside a showing of *Attack of the Clones*. Armand had come to my rescue, played it cool, apologized loudly for being late and sneaked me out the back exit to his car so I could cry in private. Two days later Jeremy's wallet went missing, his jerk-off pic and $100, plus he had to pony up another $25 for a new student ID. We went out for steaks at The Farmhouse with that $100. We buried the wallet to prove we were buccaneers not to be messed with.

A porch light came on. We froze. My heart was in my throat. A loud voice carried on a one-sided conversation in bright Spanish. Mr. Braun's nurse, probably chatting on the phone. My high-school memory clicked on, trying to fill in what she was saying. *Flowers . . . No Mama . . . tin dog . . . took the cornflakes . . . to school . . . ?* I was never very good at Spanish.

We heard the porch door open and close. A minute later, the light went out. "Come on," I said. "Let's divvy up our loot elsewhere."

* * *

The sun was coming up as we crawled up to the Van Owens' house. I stuffed Jeremy's wallet in their mailbox and he drove me back to my car. "You gonna be okay to drive?" he asked.

"I can always catch a nap at a rest stop," I said. "You?"

"I'll get some coffee," he said.

"You finally developed a taste for it, huh?"

"Blame that on Tessa," he said. "Text me when you get back so I know you got in safe."

"You too."

We hugged. I savored the scent of water and sunshine that was so unmistakably his. I took the photo, he kept the CD, we promised each other we'd make copies of each.

There was a dull throbbing in my temple, rum and lack of coffee, lack of sleep. At the edge of town, I stopped and bought a bag of ginger chews. I peeled off the wrapper like I was undressing a lover. I sucked on my past the whole drive home.

Dark 'n Stormy®

REPRESENTING BERMUDA IN OUR AROUND the world trip is the Dark 'n Stormy. Legally, there is only one way to make a Dark 'n Stormy: Pour one and a half ounces of Gosling's Black Seal® Rum into a highball glass, fill with ice, top it off with ginger beer, garnish with lime. If you put the drink on the menu at your bar, you have to do it like that—it's a proprietary recipe, like the Pusser's Painkiller.

But if you're home, and you just happen to have any sort of dark or golden rum on hand, and if you happen to think squeezing a more generous portion of lime into the drink enhances the flavor, *and* if you also happen to think grating a bit of fresh ginger into the mix perks it up . . . well, no one would ever know, now would they? Of course, I'm not advising you to do this, simply telling you it's an option for aesthetic adventurers like yourself. I'm not the boss of you, nor am I able to give legal advice, except to tell you to do as thou wilt. As always, that is the whole of the law.

Ingredients

1½ oz. Gosling's Black Seal® Rum

Ginger beer

Lime wedge, to garnish

How to Make It: As I said, put 1½ ounces of Gosling's Black Seal® Rum in a highball glass with ice. Top with ginger beer, garnish with a lime wedge. Any alterations or experimentations beyond that are on you, dear reader.

Two Americans Walk Into a Pub . . .

by Maurice Broaddus

LUCIUS AND SCOTT BRADEN WANDERED into a little pub over in Battersea. Red lions embossed the menus and the glass partition separating the bar from the open seating area. The Heptones' "Baby (Be True)" played from the speakers. Union Jacks hung all about like pennants between the televisions ringing the bar. People angled themselves to watch the soccer games, horse races, boxing matches, or cricket matches, keeping their allegiances to themselves as they silently drank. Slot machines huddled near the back. This was the place.

"Everything in England smells like the twelfth century." Lucius nudged his glasses up along the bridge of his nose. He fanned himself with his Stanford baseball cap, making sure everyone noticed it.

A woman, easily in her mid sixties and acting like the Queen of Jamaicans, held court while tending bar. Her thick plaits wove into a ponytail. A light blue sundress with a floral pattern showed off matronly arms, the kind with pouches of flab that jiggled when she moved. She still had the legs to pull off her calf-high leather boots.

The bartender wrapped up a ribald poem recital, ". . . 'Let fart be free wherever you be. For this was the end of poor Mary Lee.'"

About thirty men sitting around the bar, a mix of Jamaican and British accents, erupted in laughter, the way petrified employees do when the CEO makes a joke.

Catching the bartender's eye, Scott pointed with his chin toward the back. She nodded in return. "What's up, Honey Boo Boo?" Scott said when he passed the lone white guy at the bar. The scraggily-looking man cut a sideways glance back at Scott, but either not getting the reference or not caring, put his glass to his lips.

At the next table over, a young boy was drawing cartoons.

"What's up li'l man? What's good?" Scott asked.

The boy didn't respond. He—the bartender, too, for that matter—had a complexion Grandma Braden would've called "high yella." A big-headed boy. Scott expected his head to bobble whenever he moved. The boy hunched over a stack of *Judge Dredd* comic books and avoided their eyes.

"Dude, he all right to be in here?" Scott asked.

"Drinking age is sixteen over here," Lucius said.

"He looks eight."

"He's twelve. My grandson." Like a light switch had been flicked, the bartender's accent sounded less pronounced, like a teacher who slowed her speech for those who couldn't keep up. "He goes to school in Brixton and takes the bus out here to wait till I get off work. What'll you two have?"

"We're looking for the true British experience." Lucius raised his glasses to scan a nearby menu.

"You're looking for the true British experience . . . in gentrified London?" the bartender asked. "Do you mean like eating fish 'n chips in front of Big Ben?"

"I know. I hate it when he says stuff like that. I don't know what he means by that," Scott said, ingratiating himself at his brother's expense. "Like we expect to be roofied, and wake up being buggered by Winnie the Pooh for an audience of Beefeaters."

"I'll know it when I see it. You go ahead and order." Lucius picked up his phone. "I'm gonna look up the most popular drink in England."

The bartender sighed. "It's tea."

"Okay, alcoholic drink." Lucius typed into his cell phone.

"Guinness, then," the bartender said.

"I'll have me a Guinness, mate," Scott said in an affected voice.

"Don't do that," Lucius scolded. "Your accent qualifies as hate speech."

The bartender rolled her eyes and left. She returned with a tall glass and slid it to Scott. He slurped the foam head.

"What about you?" she asked.

"Do you serve food?" Lucius asked.

"If you're hungry, I can send my grandson to run and get you a curry."

"But, I want something truly—"

"Truly British?" the bartender finished. "Steak and kidney pie?"

Lucius made a buzzer noise. "No organs for lunch."

"You're the first in line for mom's chittlins at Thanksgiving," Scott said.

"Scotch eggs? Bangers and mash? Bubble and Squeak?" the bartender asked.

"None of those even sound like food. I'll just do fish and chips."

The boy rose and took up a position next to his grandmother. He touched the spongy flesh at her elbow like it reassured him. The bartender narrowed her shrewd eyes. "Ten pounds. Maybe when he gets back, you'll have made up your mind."

The bartender returned to her post and turned to her small television behind the bar. Big Daddy fought some kind of British hillbilly calling himself Giant Haystacks in a replay of an apparently classic bout. "Daddy!" she yelled, imitating one of his signature moves, driving her elbow into an invisible opponent.

"Did I tell you I got this text message that says 'From Debra'?" Scott sipped his Guinness. "I'm all beaming with pride cause my baby girl is checking in though I'm out of the country. Then it's this selfie . . . naked from the neck down. Check it out!"

Lucius jerked away from the phone and threw up his arms. "Dude! I can't see that. That's my niece."

"I know, right? That's what I thought. I'm all like she done confused my number with some random dude's. I've failed as a father all the way around. Next stop, she's a stripper and calling herself Krystal. I might as well kill myself."

"You can't just go around showing that to people. That's just . . . wrong."

"Anyway, turns out it was this girl I had just started talking to. I forgot her name was Debra, too."

"For real?" Lucius leaned forward. "Let me see that again."

The boy returned and handed a sack to his grandmother. The boy went to his table to break open his steak and kidney pie, the bartender on his heels to deliver the fish and chips.

"This must weigh twenty pounds." Lucius hefted the sack a few times.

"It's mostly grease," Scott said.

"They used to serve it on newspaper," the bartender said.

"I guess people started caring about inky fries." Lucius caught her eye. "Your *chips* look like half a potato," Scott said. "Don't know why everyone can't speak English. I mean, American."

The bartender pulled a remote control from her dress pocket and changed all the mounted televisions to *Danger Mouse*. She turned up the sound. The men around the bar sighed. She cut her eyes at them and they kept on drinking.

"What's up with the *Danger Mouse*?" Scott asked through a mouthful of his brother's chips.

"It's his favorite cartoon," the bartender said.

"No one minds?"

"Not after the first time I ignored their complaints." The bartender tapped her notepad.

"Man, daddy could work miracles with some catfish." Lucius poked at the breaded fish. "Can I get some white bread and hot sauce with this?"

"No." She picked up a bottle of malt vinegar. "You like this?"

"I've never understood vinegar on fries."

Staring him directly in his eyes, she splashed some on his food.

"Hah! She punked you," Scott said.

Lucius picked up a piece of vinegar-coated fish, eyeing it suspiciously. He chewed, considering the bite. Then he nodded and added more to his fish.

"Make up your mind about a drink?" she asked.

"Any suggestions?" Lucius asked.

"How about a Pimm's Cup?"

"Pimp's Cup?" Scott chimed in.

"Pimm's Cup." The bartender sucked her teeth. "Pimm's Number One, ginger ale, cucumber, strawberry, orange, and lemon slices. Plus some mint leaves."

"Sounds more like a salad than a drink," Scott said.

"People throwing mint into drinks. Like that mess they drink at the Kentucky Derby," Lucius said.

"It's refreshing. A must at cricket matches." The bartender sounded like she was reciting from a script she'd lost interest in. "I'm sure you two must be charming back home, but do you want the drink or not?"

Lucius nodded, but didn't quite meet her eyes.

"Can you at least serve it in a pimp cup?" Scott asked.

"No." The bartender returned to the bar. She returned with a tall glass filled with fruit, ice, and reddish liquid. Without comment, she slid it, and a bill, to him.

"It looks like a mutant sangria." Lucius took a tentative sip. He screwed up his face, swishing the mouthful about like he was making up his mind. He focused on the condensation along his highball glass. He wiped the glass with his napkin before he kept drinking.

"Are you drunk right now? You've got your drunk face on," Scott said.

"It *is* refreshing." Lucius gave a thumbs-up to the bartender. She turned back to her wrestling.

"You're lucky she didn't spit it in. I don't think she likes you."

"Me? You're the obnoxious one." Lucius drained the glass and pushed away from the table. He dropped money on the receipt to cover the bill.

The boy glanced up and watched them leave. So did the white man, who called out, "Enjoy your lady's drinky-winky, did you, young miss?" at Lucius's back.

The bartender smirked as she wiped down their table. "Bloody Americans."

Pimm's Cup

ANYONE FOR PIMM'S? REPRESENTING ENGLAND we have the Pimm's Cup, that iconic, oh-so-English drink that, when made properly, should immediately make you feel like you're lounging around in a lawn chair, wondering aloud to your companions if it will rain, while the more athletically inclined members of your party play cricket. Part fruit salad, part tonic, part cocktail, there's nothing out there quite like a Pimm's.

Why is the Pimm's Cup so perfect for the summer? Well, it uses many aromatic summer garden favorites like strawberries, cucumbers, and mint. The liquor itself plays well with lemonade, another summer favorite. And its relatively low alcohol content means you can knock back a few without getting too drunk in the hot summer sun.

It's true that a proper Pimm's cup is about as much prep work as you'd put into a meal, with all the chopping and peeling and whatnot. In my opinion it's best to cut up enough vegetation at the start of your afternoon so you're not fiddling with coring strawberries when you'd rather be relaxing into the evening with your fourth or fifth of these delightful concoctions.

Ingredients

Lemon wedge

Orange wedge

Strawberries, sliced

Mint sprig

2 oz. Pimm's No. 1

2 oz. lemonade

2 oz. ginger beer or ginger ale (ginger beer preferred)

Cucumber spear (English cucumber preferred)

How to Make It: In a tall glass, squeeze in your lemon and orange wedges, and toss them in with the strawberries and mint. Muddle them a bit, then pour in the Pimm's, lemonade, and ginger beer. Stir it all up with some ice cubes (not too many if you want to be *really* English about it) and garnish with the cucumber spear—just slide it right down the side of the glass.

You can also make a Pimm's Cup with champagne or sparkling wine, a drink called a Pimm's Royal or Royale. I'd still suggest using a bit of lemonade because lemon is very nice with the Pimm's.

Sangria

SANGRIA IS A DRINK OF Spanish origin, though Wikipedia tells me the name might be of Sanskrit origin. Weird! I always thought it was from the Spanish "sangre" ("blood") but it could be "sakkari," Urdu for "sugared wine." Is there nothing we can't almost learn from the Internet?

No matter where the word itself comes from, Sangria is flippin' delicious when done right. Yes, when done right. All too often Sangria is served as a really *really* sweet beverage, loaded with sugar and then more sugar via fruit juices or even fruit juice "cocktails"— you know, the type that claim to have "real fruit juice" but are really just mostly water and some sort of fruity concentrate. I'm not saying I've never gotten shitty on that type of Sangria, and happily so, but we can do better. We *deserve* better.

Ingredients

1 bottle wine (red or white; just make sure it's inexpensive but not cheap)

1 to 3 oz. decent cognac, brandy, or rum

1 to 3 oz. fruit liqueur, such as Cointreau

Chopped fruits of your choice
Seltzer water or citrus soda

How to Make It: Sangria is really more a method than a recipe. It's hard to mess it up! Basically, start with decent wine—something you'd drink on its own, but nothing too expensive. Around ten bucks is fine. For reds, I usually pick a Pinot Noir or a Red Zinfandel, but sure, you could do a Spanish red wine like a Grenache. For whites, stick to something like a Pinot Grigio or Sauvignon Blanc. Riesling is too sweet and that oaky flavor of Chardonnay clashes with sweet fruits.

Pour your wine into a nice jug, then add in your cognac and orange liqueur. I usually do Cointreau but you could do Grand Marnier or even something like Chambord, if you're using a lot of summer berries. I prefer Cointreau because it's sweet, but not too sweet.

Then, add your chopped fruit. I like to do a nice mix of fruits—some citrus, some noncitrus. Check what's cheap at the store, basically. I've found it doesn't matter what type of wine you're using—any fruit will do with any wine. So, if strawberries are in season, use those! Peaches, plums, and other stone fruit are also awesome in Sangria, as are apples. I stay away from limes, as they can become bitter, but grapefruit chunks, orange wedges, or lemon wheels are great. I have also sometimes used Sangria as a way to use up whatever fruit is languishing in the back of my freezer from whenever I last promised myself that this time I'd really start to make smoothies for breakfast. A Sangria made with freezer-burned mango chunks, blueberries, and an old orange from the back of the fridge will be very nearly as delicious as a Sangria made from those organic peaches you picked up from the farmers' market.

Dump in a few cups of fruit, and then stir it all up with a nice long spoon. Then, cover the jug with a lid or plastic wrap, and stick it in your fridge for a few hours. You *must* let it sit. I know, I know. But trust me, it's worth it.

When your Sangria has macerated enough, stir it all again, and serve with a splash of something sparkling on top. Plain seltzer is great, especially if your fruits were super sweet, but if you end up with a tarter Sangria, feel free to sweeten it with soda. One of the best Sangrias I ever made was with lemon-lime Original New York Seltzer, which is apparently not seltzer water, but soda. Happy accident! Some say you can also use sparkling wine to add a bit of fizz, and sure, but I actually like to cut my Sangria with something nonalcoholic, to reduce the chances I or my guests will get too tipsy too quickly.

Day Drinking: The Editors' Inspiration

. . . .

Some stories are simply meant to be read while the sun is still out and the light of day makes everything seem more cheerful. Same with cocktails.

Bloody at Mazie's Joint

by Benjamin Percy

Y OU HAVE TO KNOW THE way to The Underground. It's not in the yellow pages, not on the Internet. There are no signs. GPS doesn't recognize the many gravel and rut-roads that lead past the farms and through the forest to get there—to the bar cut into the side of a hill and topped by trees. The roots of an old oak frame the doorway. The walls are stone and soil framed by railroad ties. The air smells like creosote and earthworms.

The floor is a splintery mess of peanut shells. Christmas lights thread the ceiling and offer just enough light to maze my way through the scarred picnic tables and approach the bar.

Mazie waits for me here. She doesn't know me, but I know about her, like so many other women who visit this place, who drive here from all over the Midwest seeking her help.

She could be forty or sixty. She keeps her gray-black hair cut short. She wears a T-shirt advertising the Packers. She has thick forearms and big hands good for ripping the caps off beer bottles and breaking up fights. The right side of her face is mottled and discolored, as if she blew a bubble that burst and stuck to her cheek. People say it was a parting gift from an ex-husband, a trucker from Omaha. He grabbed her by the hair and lowered her face onto the woodstove.

People say that's why she wears her hair short. People say that's why she killed him.

A crossbow hangs behind her, centered on the wall and framed on all sides by shelves of whiskey and rum and vodka and gin. Rumor has it she shot a bolt through his eye and he dropped like a stone.

And if that's true, then maybe this next part is, too.

She keeps his head in a back room. Preserved in a big glass jar full of vodka. The bolt juts out of the socket. His skin has gone yellow with age. His hair wafts about his face like seaweed and his mouth hangs open to reveal a line of serrated teeth.

Mazie is big but he was bigger. And bad-tempered. People say they saw Mazie around town with a pouched black eye or her arm in a sling, and whenever anybody asked, "How did that happen?" she said, "Ran into a door," or "Got up in the middle of the night to use the bathroom and tripped over the laundry basket."

And here's the thing. The most important thing about The Underground, and the dead husband, and the severed head floating in a jar of vodka. Mazie is known for making a signature Bloody Mary.

The bar top is a wide plank of ash, polished from years of elbows and spilled beer, and when you order the Bloody, you're supposed to knock on it—slowly—three times. Mazie will stop whatever else she's doing. Wiping a glass with a rag. Tidying the bottles on the shelf. Knifing the foam off a tap beer. She'll stop and she'll narrow her eyes and she'll lean toward you and say, "Sure about that? It takes a while. And it's costly."

That's what she says to me right now. She wants me to think twice about what I've asked. Because once it's done, there's no going back. She doesn't need the dirty details about why I'm here. Maybe someone beat me, cheated on me, sued me. It's none of her business. She assumes I'm here because I've been wronged. And I have.

"A Bloody is just the thing I need," I say.

"All right," she says, "but I can't make it without your help."

She needs something from me. A photo. A lock of hair. Fingernail clippings. An individualized ingredient. The residue of the person I want dead. I open up my hand and drop a half-spent cigarette on the bar.

"That'll do," she says and sweeps it into a pint glass.

Then she limes the rim, dirties it with black pepper, pours a can of V8 inside, adds five ice cubes, a dill pickle, a stalk of celery, a jerky stick, a spoonful of horseradish, a splash of Worcestershire, two hits of Tabasco, and then she'll disappear through the door behind the bar. That's where the magic happens. That's where she spigots three shots from the jar of vodka.

Some people say that once you take a sip of that Bloody, it takes twenty-four hours for the curse to take effect, and other people say it can take as long as a week. A heart attack or a car crash. A fall down the stairs. A horse's hoof to the head. An embolism that makes one eye go ruby red. However it happens, whoever wronged you will die.

Mazie returns from the back room and sets down a cocktail napkin and centers the Bloody on it. "There you have it. I hope you enjoy."

"I don't know if that's the right word," I say and strangle my fingers around the glass, "but it's what I need, if you know what I mean."

"I think I do," she says. "Travel far to get here?"

"Not too far," I say. "Omaha."

I hoist the glass in a toast and relish a sip—a burning sip of the Bloody Mary that contains a cigarette butt fished out of Mazie's car's ashtray.

Her eyes widen then, studying me with recognition. Her voice comes out as a whisper when she says, "Thought you looked familiar."

I gulp down another swallow. "People always said my brother and I had the same eyes, but we also shared the same bad temper. And cruel sense of humor."

Bloody Mary

THE POOR BLOODY MARY, VICTIM of these times of boredom and overindulgence. Once a perfectly reasonable fluid accompaniment to a relaxing brunch, the Bloody Mary has mutated into a meal of its own; a smorgasbord of unnecessary excess. Social media is full of horrifying pictures of Bloody Marys proudly and grotesquely garnished with enough pickles to give an individual instant, acute hypertension; an ocean's worth of innocent sea creatures; slices of bacon; whole sliders (including bun!); pizza rolls; corn dogs; grilled cheese sandwiches; entire slices of pizza. A human head steeping in the vodka seems downright reasonable, compared with that.

As we all know, the only thing necessary for the triumph of evil is for good men to do nothing, so stand up and do your part by vowing to concoct only sane Bloody Marys from this day forward. Impress your friends and guests with a beverage made from fresh ingredients in sensible proportions—not one from a mix, seasoned with rehydrated garlic, despair, and clam juice. Don't hide the elegant way vodka, tomato, and lemon come together under absurd garnishes; don't serve a drink that will just get all melty and disgusting while you eat your way through skewers holding an entire day's worth of calories. If you like spice, go ahead and spice it up reasonably with Tabasco or maybe Sriracha; avoid "extreme" hot sauces that will add absurd amounts of heat but no flavor to your drink. If you like the aromatic note of a celery top, sure, use one to add scent and color. Love olives? Put one in there, why not. Just keep in mind that there's no need to go crazy. And for goodness sake, serve any accompanying snacks on a plate.

Ingredients
1½ oz. vodka
3 oz. tomato juice
Juice of ½ a lemon
1–2 dashes Worcestershire sauce
Black pepper, to taste
Celery, for garnish
Olive, for garnish
Pickles, for garnish

How to Make It: Stir all ingredients with ice in a highball glass, then crack the pepper over the surface. Garnish sensibly with celery, an olive, or one or two pickles. Enjoy.

Josie Russell

(For a Pitcher That Serves 2–3)

CREATED BY ERNEST HEMINGWAY AND named for the man who would go on to found the famed Key West bar Sloppy Joe's, this drink has become deservedly popular in the wake of the publication of Phillip Greene's cleverly named *To Have and Have Another*. While at first the beverage seems a bit random—limes and rum make sense together, but . . . apples?—the ingredients come together in a heavenly manner. The tartness of the lime is summery, but the caramel of the rum mixed with the hint of apple flavor makes this a perfect thing to serve during a late summer's barbecue when the promise of autumn is in the air.

Hemingway's original recipe calls for sugar, rather than simple syrup, but I find Hemingway's drinks all too sour by far. Plus, why struggle to dissolve sugar—all that stirring!—when you can just use simple syrup. Select a dry, English-style cider (or even a dry perry) when making this; stay away from the sorts of sugary ciders one drinks in college when one dislikes beer but still wishes to be sociable.

(This is not a judgment on those ciders or their drinkers; it's just the wrong choice for this cocktail.)

Ingredients
4½ oz. golden rum
12 oz. hard apple cider
2 oz. fresh lime juice
1 oz. simple syrup

How to Make It: In a pitcher, combine all ingredients with lots of ice. Stir; serve in Collins or highball glasses. It's perfectly fine to double this or even triple it for a crowd, but keep in mind, this is not a light cocktail, no matter how refreshing it may seem.

Punch

PUNCH—REAL PUNCH, NOT VILE CONCOCTIONS of Kool-Aid and grain alcohol—is at long last coming back into fashion, thank goodness. This is in part due to David Wondrich's wonderful and popular book *Punch: The Delights (and Dangers) of the Flowing Bowl*, and in part due to the eagerness of hero bartenders to revive that which has been nearly lost to time. The fantastic bar Church in Portland, Oregon, always has a punch for its patrons (sitting out, as is proper, and then topped off with cold sparkling wine to keep the fizz in it); others are also realizing the power of a good punch.

Punch is great for a large party, as long as you have or purchase small cups for your guests and warn them of the drink's potency. Punch like this—a fruity riff on the famous Regent's Punch—is powerful stuff, especially with the black tea in it. Though it's drier than many punches you may have imbibed at awful campus parties, it's still tasty, sparkly, and sweet, and can get you into trouble if you don't imbibe moderately.

I like to serve my punch in one of those sun tea-style dispensers with the little spout—non-traditional, yes, but there's also less potential for disaster than with your maiden aunt's antique cut glass bowl and party cups, especially when the punch really starts to flow. Put everything save the bubbly in there, with orange slices and an ice hemisphere or ring made with a mixture of black tea and orange juice, and set out a chilled bottle of champagne in a bucket beside it. (The recipe takes two, so be a good host or hostess, keep an eye on the level of your bottle, and replace as needed.)

An ice ring can be made in any bundt cake pan or Jello mold. As my sun tea dispenser won't accommodate a big ring like that, I usually pour my tea and orange juice into a small bowl and freeze that overnight. The bigger the ice chunk, the slower it will melt.

Ingredients
1 pint black tea
12 oz. sugar

One 12 oz. bag of frozen raspberries, thawed
Thin cut rinds of 4 lemon(s)
6 oz. fresh lemon juice (from the peeled lemons)
1½ cups orange juice
1 pint good brandy
½ pint golden rum
Slices of orange(s)
2 bottles Brut champagne

How to Make It: The morning of your party, make a pint of good, strong black tea. Use four to five teaspoons of black, unflavored loose-leaf tea, like an Assam or a Yunan. If you don't have a big enough teapot, do it in a pot on the stove by making a big tea bag out of cheesecloth with plenty of room for the tea to expand. While it should be strong (hence the overdose of tea-to-water for you tea drinkers)—don't oversteep it—go for five minutes at most. Fish out your tea bag, and while it's still hot, add the sugar, the raspberries, and the lemon peels, and steep those all day in the fridge.

Strain the mixture well, getting out all peels and seeds and pulp, and pour that into your punch bowl or dispenser. Add to that the lemon and orange juice, brandy, rum, orange slices, and if you like a colder punch, your ice, if you're using it. Place your champagne to the side in an ice bucket, and wait for the compliments to roll in.

Gin Is Stronger than Witchcraft

by Dominica Phetteplace

I WASN'T LOOKING FOR A cocktail, I was looking for a magic spell. But there were more bartenders than witches in San Francisco. Everyone either worked in tech or they worked in food. When I was married, I used to say that I was my own job. But now that I'm divorced, I just say that I'm divorced.

Cocktail class took place on the upper floor of a culinary school that catered to tech professionals. It had the word "maker" in it, or rather "makr." Vowels were like gluten or monogamy or voice-mail, useless things treasured by old people. The culinary school had classes on grilling, hot sauce, and pour-over coffee. They had a 3-D printer that used edible materials. They offered a very popular seminar on sandwiches.

I was going away to a summer camp, but before that I needed a love potion. Cocktail class seemed like the best place to find one.

Women of leisure such as myself have our choice of summer camps. I could have gone to witch camp or surf camp. I could have attended a meditation retreat. But I badly needed to win at something, and a writer's retreat seemed like something I could do well at.

I wasn't much of a writer, but neither are most writers. It seemed like a vocation you could pick up at any time. I was introverted, I had made poor life choices; I was almost there. A stint at a writer's retreat would help. So would having sex with an actual writer.

I had chosen a residency in New Hampshire that was famous for its orgies. Not that they don't have orgies in San Francisco, but the city is so small there was always the chance of running into someone you used to be married to.

I came to cocktail class with a list of love potion ingredients taken from my favorite witch forum.

"Today we're going to learn how to make a gimlet," said our instructor. She was a muscular lady, stylish in that San Francisco way: bad haircut, beautiful tattoos.

I immediately raised my hand and handed her my printed-out list. Caraway, cardamom, cinnamon, strawberries, topaz, and more.

"We're not using any of these things," she said. Then she launched into a three-hour class on how to make a gimlet. Just a gimlet, nothing else. I'd thought a cocktail class would teach us how to make many cocktails, but I underestimated the fussiness of Bay Area foodie culture. One cocktail, three hours, four hundred dollars.

"The gimlet is a very versatile drink. It can be made with five-dollar gin," said the teacher.

My classmates scoffed at this. Only the homeless drank cheap liquor.

"It can also be made with vodka. If you make it with rum, then it's a daiquiri." The gimlet was traditionally made with lime juice, but other citruses could be substituted. Grapefruit was recommended. So was orange. The most important thing was that you used a fresh-squeezed juice.

"Citrus juice begins to lose its potency and flavor as soon as it is squeezed." The best bartenders kept a bowl of whole fruit by the bar.

We were instructed on how to chill beakers and glasses. We were instructed on how to stir and why. Shaking "bruises" the alcohol, we were told. Our instructor had plenty to say about every single aspect of gimlet making. It was actually pretty boring, and after three hours I was ready to leave. When she finally dismissed the class, I was the first one to stand up.

But she pointed right at me and told me to stay after.

"You," she said. "Are you trying to make a love spell or a sex spell?" She showed me the tattoo on the inside of her wrist. It was some runic-looking thing that I pretended to recognize. I wasn't any sort of expert. I was a casual witch. An Internet witch. I got my spells from Twitter. I wore a lot of black, but only on overcast days.

"A gimlet can be adapted into a love spell with the addition of geranium bitters."

"That sounds gross, actually," I said.

"I'd recommend orange juice if you're looking for a sex spell . . ."

"Orange?" I asked. She began to ream an orange; she was making a drink.

"Yes, to activate the second chakra. But because orange is sweet, you need to add something bitter." She added an ounce of red vermouth and a few hearty dashes of orange bitters.

"Make sure you stir in the pattern of a limaçon. Imagine a flower blossoming. Intent is very important."

"Why are you telling me all of this?" I asked. She raised an eyebrow in response. This is how women in the Bay Area signaled sexual availability, that and eyeliner. Her eyeliner game was tight, but I had always been heterosexual, even in college.

She finished mixing the drink and then poured herself a glass.

"None for me?" I asked. She shook her head no. The implication was that her potion would work. I thought it likelier that it wouldn't and that she didn't want me to know.

Witchcraft would be more compelling to me if it were reliable. The spells I did always seemed about as effective as making a wish. And yet still I tried. The advantage of a cocktail as magic spell was that as long as the drink tasted good, you had something to show for your effort no matter what.

At the retreat, I waited for a full moon to unveil my version of the orange blossom. I made it the way my instructor did, only stronger. I rubbed the rim of each glass with the inside of an orange peel so you would inhale the orange scent before taking a drink. I set my intent: *May each of us be brave enough to receive affection.* My incantation may have lacked ambition, but magic seemed to work best if you kept your expectations low.

We gathered in the main hall. We sipped our orange blossoms and stared at the expanse of floor ahead of us. Music with a strong beat blared. I decided that the empty floor in front of us was actually a dance floor. So I began to dance. It might have been my spellcraft, it might have been the gin, it might have been my dance moves, but something convinced the others to join me. First the poets, then the fiction writers, and finally the memoirists.

No orgy ensued. I went to bed early, and no one knocked at my door in the middle of the night, begging to fuck me.

The next morning, at breakfast, I asked if there were any hookups or make outs. Several people blushed and exchanged glances. There was a code of silence around these things, I could tell. Gossip was abundant everywhere except the breakfast table.

Someone changed the subject to my dance prowess. I received compliments and high fives. This had never happened to me before, not even at dance camp three summers ago. I don't even think of myself as possessing a certain set of "moves," but the others were able to recreate certain movements and ascribe them to me. I didn't really remember dancing like that, but that doesn't mean it didn't happen.

So I won something. I won the dance party at the writer's retreat. I won. The point of life isn't to win everything, but neither is it to always lose. Winning is like drinking. You should win the right things, and in the right amounts. And crafting drinks is like crafting spells: something bitter and something sweet will help to awaken the right spirit.

Orange Blossom

THE ORANGE BLOSSOM USED TO contain sweet vermouth; these days, when you order one you'll usually get something more like a gin screwdriver. I love the taste of Italian vermouth, and the resulting rich flavor is, to me, worth how the addition turns the drink an admittedly unaesthetic shade of muddy orange-brown. Well, we can't all be beautiful.

Ingredients
1 oz. London dry gin
1 oz. fresh squeezed orange juice, strained
1 oz. Italian sweet vermouth
Orange bitters
Maraschino cherry, to garnish

How to Make It: In a cocktail shaker, add all ingredients except for the garnish. Stir with lots of ice until cold; strain into a cocktail glass, and garnish with a cherry. If you use store-bought orange juice for this, which, you know, happens, make sure it's pulp-free by nature or by straining it unless you want the drink to be chunky as well as hideous.

Mint Julep Through the Ages

by Jim Nisbet

TAMMY AND I CONCEIVED A mutual crush on a rehearsal break during which, having discovered we were both from the south and therefore supposed to like mint juleps, and having further discovered the back door to a so-called pocket bar directly across the alley from the stage door outside of which Tammy liked to smoke a cigarette while the director obsessed over the blocking of lighting cues in scenes for which he'd demanded rewrites yet to materialize, we ordered one with two straws because, after all, we were working. And lo and behold the bartender said, "You know, I haven't served a mixed drink in this shithole since the Nixon administration, when all the theater folk that came in here wanted boilermakers on account they were so depressed by Henry Kissinger's accent." He waggled a thumb at the ceiling. "Among other things."

Tammy deployed her rubber features by way of communicating puzzlement. "A boilermaker is a mixed drink?"

"It is in here," the bartender said, "but the real problem," he added, " is, I got no mint."

"Danny." Tammy didn't miss a beat, and she didn't even look at me. "Be a darlin' and go find this man some mint."

The bartender paused the desiccation of a nervous glass to look at Tammy, blink, then look at me.

"I'll wait here," Tammy added.

Fast forward, a kebab joint down the street had a sprig of mint, and Bartender made a delicious one-pint mint julep. Straws, he had. Ice, too, a miracle. High-octane bourbon, sugar, etc. Tammy and I chased each other around backstage, knocked over a stack of flats, got fired, never saw each other again. You were expecting consummation? She had a live-in boyfriend, I was a nobody, etc., etc. But the main thing is, as I caught up with her and we wrapped ourselves in a leg, stage right, "Danny," Tammy warned, as we broke off a long kiss, "once I fuck you, you stay fucked."

"Hey!" said the stage manager, who looked more like a railroad bull than an *artiste*, "what the fuck you two think you're doin' back here?"

Forty-two point six years later, I ran into Tammy at a country club bar in Tucson. Not that I recognized her, at first, nor she me. Au contraire. I took one look at this broad, thumbing the screen of her cellphone, next stool over and, okay, I admit, I gave her a second thought, which was, *In all my earthly sojourn, I've never seen so much plastic surgery.*

But then, as I was thinking that thought, the bartender (a different bartender) appeared and asked what she wanted. This distorted visage looked up from its phone, blinked at the bartender, turned for a look at me, blinked again and said, "Oh, I don't know." She turned back to the bartender. "What about a mint julep?"

Immediately, I recognized the voice.

Unfazed by the request, the bartender ignored me and went about his business, no round trip to the kebab joint involved. My neighbor went back to her phone.

I took advantage. She'd always been short, okay, she was still short. Her hair was still dirty blonde, with highlights, curled or whatever—permed?—but, still, much as I remembered it. In any case, it wasn't half-gray like mine. Okay, two-thirds. Showing, I mean. We're in Tucson, it's 110 degrees outside, they got air-conditioning figured out in Tucson like no place I've ever been, so her T-shirt is okay outside and it's okay inside, no sweater over the shoulders in case there's icicles on the supply vent. But it's not just any T-shirt, it's a really cool T-shirt, piping around the sleeves and the sleeves are very short, she's been toning at the gym, there's no logo discernible on it, and it fits her like . . . like . . .

"Here you are, Mrs. Myers." The bartender centered a drink in a pewter cup on a napkin in front of her. It had ice, there were dark green areas below the surface, a sprig of mint floated atop everything, and there was a single fat black straw. "Will there be anything else?"

"Another straw," I said.

They both looked at me.

"Danny," Tammy said. She didn't even look at the bartender. "Another straw, please."

The guy went away.

Tammy glanced at her drink, then leveled her gaze at me. "I haven't had a mint julep in thirty years."

"It's probably more like forty-two point six." I shrugged. "Either way, I don't blame you."

The bartender returned. We ignored him. He lay a black straw across Tammy's coaster and went away.

We took a moment to absorb each other's years—impossible, of course. But what's the choice? Screaming?

"So you're alive." Tammy toyed with the straw without picking it up.

"Apparently."

"Unlike Tucson," she added.

I cast a glance around the room. In fact, the guy I'd intended to meet had yet to show, and he was late enough to make me think he wasn't going to show at all. Oh well. The fee for driving a hot car from Tucson to LA, even if it's an expensive hot car, isn't that much. Really, it depends on how bad you want to be in LA. And since I was clean, truth to tell? I should have been heading the other way. But they don't pay people to drive expensive cars to chop shops in Ft. Wayne. Maybe they don't have any?

"I like peace and quiet," I told her.

She lifted the straw, turned it this way and that, then slowly sank its length into my side of her mint julep. "Thirsty?" she asked.

I leaned in and took a long pull. "No," I said, straightening up. The chilled bourbon felt like molten gold going down a tungsten esophagus: top-shelf metallurgy.

As Tammy took a dainty sip from her own straw, her phone bleeped. "My surgeon." She smiled and touched the screen. The phone went silent.

"Oh," I said. "Is everything . . . ?"

"Everything is fine." She placed the phone facedown on the bar.

"Oh," I began, and fell silent by way of not launching into how glad I was to hear it on account I'd been knowing a lot of dead people lately.

Tammy cupped her breasts through the T-shirt and lifted them. "The girls are looking better than ever." She jostled her breasts. "Hardly even sore." She smiled sleepily. "Taut, even."

"Has," I thought to ask, "the anesthetic worn off?"

"Oh," Tammy assured me, "it's an outpatient procedure. Strictly local."

"Really?"

"You get to watch?"

I blinked aloud.

Tammy smiled. "Didn't we meet in a theater?"

That was true. But, "A long time ago," I pointed out.

"You got to get the right guy," she confirmed. "Did you notice this?" She held out her left hand.

"Wow. That's a big . . . I mean, it's a . . . beautiful . . . rock."

Turning her curled fingers so she could admire the ring herself, Tammy revived the sleepy smile. "He's a geologist."

I took a moment to absorb this.

"Don't you like our mint julep?" Tammy took a sip.

I took a sip.

Our noses touched.

"Did the geologist dig up your surgeon, too?"

"Oh no. He leaves that stuff to me."

"But he likes the results?"

Tammy smiled. "He likes the results."

"The girls," I quoted.

"The girls," Tammy reiterated, "are like new."

She took a sip.

I took a sip.

We didn't touch noses.

I settled an elbow on the bar and the side of my head in my hand. "Show me."

Tammy didn't miss a beat. "I'm a happily married woman, Danny."

The bar was bright; it was still daylight. There were only a couple of other customers, plus the bartender. On the green beyond the patio, a foursome was putting out.

"And if you weren't happy, Tammy?"

Tammy shrugged. "It wouldn't be anything they haven't seen in here before."

I knew she'd lived in Tucson a long time. I was just a tourist.

"I wouldn't put it past you, Tammy."

Tammy nodded, the gleam of top-shelf metallurgy in her eyes. "Don't."

"I'd like to remember you like that."

Tammy smiled. "Do."

She put down her straw and called for the check.

Mint Julep

THE MINT JULEP IS ONE of the most simple, delicious, and balanced cocktails out there. And yet, there are so many terrible recipes filled with unnecessary garbage that I decided to take a stand here and advocate for the most basic interpretation of the drink.

You might think that a combination of rye and cognac must be a fancier or more modern interpretation of the julep than just bourbon, but a very old recipe for what's called the "prescription" julep features rye and cognac in combination. That recipe goes for a higher proportion of liquor to sugar and mint, but four ounces of high-proof liquor is sometimes hard to handle. I like a sweeter, mellower drink that is still flavorful, excites the senses, and gets you where you need to be.

Ingredients

Lots and lots of mint
Lots and lots of cracked ice
1 sugar cube
1 tbsp. water

1½ oz. rye whiskey (preferred) or bourbon whiskey

1½ oz. cognac

How to Make It:

This recipe is a little complex, so here's a numbered list of steps.

1. Begin by picking and washing lots of fresh mint—several handfuls at least. I actually keep a mint plant for mint juleps. Store-bought is fine but mint is so easy to grow, why not do things the right way?
2. Crack lots and lots of ice in an ice crusher, or get a nice big bowl from the crusher in your freezer.
3. Put a sugar cube in the bottom of either a julep cup or any wide-mouthed drinking vessel (i.e., not a highball). Pour over the water and toss in some mint. Muddle.
4. Spread a layer of cracked ice over this concoction.
5. Bruise the mint by pressing it gently with your fingertips, and spread a layer of it over the ice.
6. Repeat layering cracked ice and mint until the glass is full.
7. Pour over this parfait your rye and your cognac. Stir.
8. Garnish with a perfect sprig of mint if you like. Some people make much hay over drinking a julep through a straw cut short so your nose is in the mint. Eh. You can do that, but you can also skip it. Sipping is just fine.

Never trust any drink recipe that calls for powdered sugar. Yes, dissolving sugar can be a pain. Yes, you must add water to do so, and it takes a few extra minutes. Yes, making simple syrup is an extra step, and it goes bad after a bit and you have to remember when you made it and then you dump it out because "when in doubt" and you feel like you wasted sugar and time. But powdered sugar contains cornstarch as an anticaking agent and will give your drinks a raw cornstarch taste, which is disgusting. Remember: doing things the right way is never the wrong choice!

Nightcaps: Recipes and Fiction for After Dark

. . . .

The fiction in this section reflects what happens when the sun sets and the shades are drawn. The cocktails are challenging, pushing the boundaries and involving some ingredients that only those brave enough to leave the light behind will find intriguing.

Dinner with the Fire Breathers

by Robert Swartwood

. . . .

A BOUT TEN MINUTES INTO MEETING Jessica's parents for the first time, her father starts to tell me about a dragon egg. Beside me on the couch, Jessica sighs. "Dad, please."

"What *please*?" A stern expression crosses his face. "There is no *please*. There is only the *truth*."

He turns back to me, a warm look in his eyes now, waving his hand around like a conductor to clear the air.

"So as I was saying, I was just a boy at the time, sixteen years old, and my troupe was passing through this small town in Russia called Artyomovsky, and there was a man there, a noble man who somehow survived Stalin with his wealth intact, who invited us to his mansion, which turned out to be a castle, and after we performed, the man was so impressed that he ushered us down into his basement where he kept—"

He cuts himself off as Jessica's mother enters the room carrying a tray of steaming beverages. Again, it hasn't even been fifteen minutes since meeting Jessica's folks for the first time, and after a quick series of awkward handshakes and hellos (I'm the guy who's been dating their daughter for two years and this is the first contact I've had with them), they led us to this parlor and asked if we'd like something to drink and while Jessica shook her head and said no, I didn't want to be rude and said that would be great.

And now here Jessica's mother comes with that silver tray. On the silver tray are four small mugs, over which, like I said, hover small clouds of steam, and my first thought is coffee.

Jessica's father rises from his chair to help his wife with the tray. He holds it while Jessica's mother takes one of the small mugs and offers it to Jessica.

Jessica says, "I told you I didn't want any."

"Jessica"—a tinge of exasperation in the older woman's voice—"don't be rude."

But Jessica doesn't appear to have any intentions of accepting the drink. The stalemate lasts only a couple seconds, and then Jessica's mother turns, forces a smile, and offers the mug to me.

I gratefully accept the drink. "Thank you," I say, and then lift the mug to my face to smell the coffee. Only it smells entirely different. "May I ask what this is?"

Jessica's mother has set another one of the small mugs on the table beside the couch for Jessica to take whenever she wants. She takes a mug for herself, Jessica's father takes a mug for himself, the silver tray is set aside and both of them sit again on their thrones.

Seriously—the chairs resemble thrones more than anything else. Then again, this shouldn't be surprising as the home is something like a mansion. An *old* mansion, to be more specific, just like from Jessica's father's story. Not just old in years, but in centuries. My first impression as I pulled into the drive was that it looked like something you'd find in Europe, not upstate Pennsylvania.

"Smoking Bishop," Jessica's mother says.

Jessica's father says, "That's the proper name, yes, but I like to think of it simply as Dragon's Breath."

Jessica sighs again.

I take a hesitant sip. It's warm, of course, but surprisingly very good. Citrusy and spicy and sweet. "What's in it?"

Jessica's mother opens her mouth, but before she can speak, her husband clears his throat.

"The reason I call it Dragon's Breath," he says, "is that it is what every fire breather in our family drinks."

Both of Jessica's parents take a sip from their mugs while I sit there wondering whether I had heard that correctly.

"I'm sorry, but did you say *fire breather*?"

"Of course," Jessica's father says. "That's what we are. That's *who* we are. I am a fire breather just as my wife is a fire breather, just as our parents were fire breathers before us, and their parents fire breathers before them."

I sneak a glance at Jessica, hoping that she'll give me a look, show me that this is just one big joke, but she sits stoically on the couch, staring down at her hands.

"I see," Jessica's father says, after a long moment. "Our daughter did not tell you about her past, did she?"

Not sure what to say, I shake my head.

"Jessica was one of the very best fire breathers in our family history," her father says. "And trust me when I tell you that you are sitting among some of the greatest fire breathers in the world."

"I'm sorry, but can you elaborate on what you mean when you say fire breather?"

Her parents stare at me, confused. As if the question I just asked was so silly it doesn't warrant a response.

Jessica whispers, "My parents are circus performers."

"We are not *circus* performers," her father growls. "We are *artists*! *Fire* artists!"

Jessica's mother says, "It broke our hearts the day Jessica told us she no longer wanted to perform. It felt"—her voice hitches—"it felt as if she was turning her back on her destiny."

"It didn't *feel* that way," Jessica's father says. "It *was* that way!"

Jessica shifts in her seat to look at me, the intensity in her eyes explosive. "We should leave."

"Why leave?" her father asks. "You came for dinner. We haven't even had dinner yet!"

"I don't want to talk about performing anymore." Jessica speaks through clenched teeth. "Why can't you get that through your heads? I don't want to talk about performing and I don't want to talk about dragon eggs and I certainly don't want to drink that shit anymore."

Her parents stare at her, stunned.

"I know you don't approve of what I do," Jessica says, "but it's my life. I'm happy."

Her father's face reddens. "You work in an office. You sit at a desk and you answer phones and sign invoices. What kind of life is that?"

"What kind of life is *that*? That's normal life! That's what normal people do! They don't tour the world spitting fire out of their mouths just to get a smattering of applause."

Somehow, her father's face reddens even more. He doesn't say anything, though, just sits there on his throne, his wife beside him, and glowers at his daughter. I notice for the first time that he doesn't really have eyebrows. Neither does his wife.

Jessica rises to her feet, looks at me. "Let's go."

We don't speak much in the car. It's a three-hour drive back to the city and the silence is palpable. Jessica sits staring out her window, her arms crossed, until suddenly she breaks the silence.

"I can't believe you talked me into setting up dinner with those people. I told you I don't talk to my parents anymore. They drive me nuts. Why can't they understand I just don't want to do what they want me to do?"

I don't answer, keeping my focus on the highway. In the left front pocket of my khakis I can feel the slight impression of the engagement ring I'd just had engraved. It'll be melted down and sold for pennyweight by the end of the month.

"It's *my* life," Jessica mumbles, turning her attention back out her window again. "*My* life."

Three years pass and I'm at a Christmas dinner party hosted by some coworkers. After Jessica, I swore off Match.com, so I'm at the party, single, drifting from one tepid conversation to another, when I find myself in the kitchen. A woman stands by the stove, using a ladle to pour something into small mugs.

"Just in time!" she says.

"In time for what?"

"An intensely sweet little pick-me-up." She hands me one of the mugs. "I bet you'll never guess what this is called."

I sniff the drink. Smell something familiar.

"It's the perfect Christmas drink," she says.

"Why's that?"

"It's from *A Christmas Carol*. Please tell me you've read *A Christmas Carol*."

"I've seen the Mister Magoo version."

She laughs. It's a soft, melodious sound that I immediately want to hear again.

"I'm Doug," I say. "And I'll take your bet."

"Sophia. And I'm pretty sure Mister Magoo didn't drink this in his movie. Now what do you want to bet?"

"Dinner with me."

She looks at me again, curious, and says, "You're on."

"Smoking Bishop," I say, matter-of-factly.

"Wow, I'm shocked."

"But I've heard it called another name once."

She frowns. "What's that?"

"Dragon's Breath." I force a smile. "It's a long story, and I never got to hear how it ended."

Smoking Bishop

SMOKING BISHOP IS A HOT punch usually served at Yuletide—indeed, it's mentioned in Dickens' venerable *A Christmas Carol*, in the scene where Scrooge, post-visitation, is finally nice to poor Bob Cratchit:

> "A merry Christmas, Bob!" said Scrooge, with an earnestness that could not be mistaken, as he clapped him on the back. "A merrier Christmas, Bob, my good fellow, than I have given you, for many a year! I'll raise your salary, and endeavour to assist your struggling family, and we will discuss your affairs this very afternoon, over a Christmas bowl of smoking bishop, Bob!"

While the Christmas connection cannot (and should not!) be ignored, Smoking Bishop is delicious on any cold night of the year. It does take a bit of prep, though, so check the forecast and begin well in advance.

As with any punch, there are a zillion recipes out there for Smoking Bishop. Some call for ginger to be added; others for more exotic spices like allspice or mace (nutmeg husk—delicious!). I like to keep things simple, so I just go for cinnamon and clove, which are at most grocery stores. And I alter the more traditional lemon/orange combination to be orange/grapefruit because originally, Saville oranges were used in this drink—the type of orange you make into marmalade. Bitter and citrusy, I think unless you can find real Saville oranges, the bitterness of the grapefruit does a lot more to enhance the drink (and balance out the sweetness of the oranges) than the pure sourness of a lemon.

Ingredients

3 oranges

2 grapefruits

25 whole cloves

1 bottle Spanish red wine (or any red wine, really)

2 cinnamon sticks

½ cup white sugar

1 bottle vintage port (or ruby, but I like vintage)

How to Make It: Wash your citrus well, removing any stickers or wax. (If you get waxed fruit, soak it in a mild vinegar solution or one of those store-bought fruit/veggie washes and then rinse.) With a paring knife, make five tiny x-shaped incisions per orange or grapefruit and insert a whole clove into each.

Set your oven to 300 degrees, then roast your citrus fruits in a glass lasagna pan, checking them after an hour. When the peels have lost their brightness, take them out—it might take a bit longer. Using tongs, take them out of the pan and put them in a deep bowl.

When your citrus is just about done, pour your red wine into a saucepan and heat very gently on the stove with the cinnamon sticks and sugar, stirring until all the sugar is dissolved. After your citrus is in your big bowl, pour the hot wine and sugar and cinnamon over the oranges. Cover that with plastic wrap and let it sit for twenty-four hours in a warm place.

After twenty-four hours, cut your citrus in half and juice them into the wine. Pour this spicy fruity wine through a fine-mesh strainer into the pot (or if you have a slow cooker that can be set to very low, a slow cooker), pressing on the solids to get out all the goodness. Add the whole bottle of port to this mixture (except the port lees, if you're using vintage) and then heat gently until it's "smoking." Be careful on the stove—you don't want to boil it!—and if you're using a slow cooker, it's fine to use the high setting for a while but make sure you set it to very low long before it boils.

Serve your Smoking Bishop in mugs or punch glasses. If you want to be fancy, put a thin slice of lemon on top. Drink and be merry.

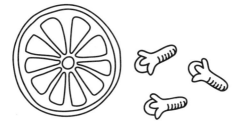

But You Can't Stay Here

by Tim Pratt

"YOU MAKE IT SOUND LIKE alchemy." Henri sprawled unmoving across most of the love seat, the untidy yards of velvet he wore attracting every cat hair in the room.

Jude poured a precise measure of dangerously infused gin into a metal shaker half full of ice. "It's chemistry, mostly, and a little bit art . . . so alchemy isn't a terrible word for it. Anyone can put a drug in a pill or a pipette. That's fine for selling at clubs and paying the bills, back when we had bills, but this is different. This is passion. I'm creating cocktails that delight or challenge the palate even as they deliver a profound psychological and physiological experience."

"You're talking like sales copy." Henri shifted on the couch, as if he might find a comfortable position, when what made him uncomfortable was his position in the world. With a listless finger he prodded the cocktail glass on the coffee table. "That last drink didn't do anything. What did you call it?"

"The New Woman. I'm sure it did what I intended. Made you feel independent, intelligent, free, and uninterested in children and family. It's just that, being a white man from an upper-middle-class background, you always feel that way anyway. It's like shining a blue spotlight on a blue wall: no contrast, no change."

Henri snorted. "That's not alchemy, that's mind control. Not that I'm complaining. Our minds could use it." He glanced at the window, closed off with heavy drapes, then resolutely looked away. "Still. Making feelings out of chemicals . . ."

"Feelings *are* chemicals," Jude said. "You're a soup of substances lit up with electricity. Chemicals are the only reason anyone does anything."

Henri put his sleeve over his face. "I never do anything."

"Chemicals are the reason for that, too."

Somewhere off to the west, where the marina had been, came a vast earth-shaking boom that rattled the windows. Neither of them mentioned it. There was no point anymore.

Jude measured in some unadulterated sweet vermouth, then picked up a bottle of dark brown liquid. The Amer Picon was key. The bitter orange liqueur had once been as common as Campari, and appeared in countless recipes from the late 19th and early 20th centuries. The liqueur had been created as a makeshift treatment for malaria by the Frenchman Gaétan Picon when he was stationed in Algiers; he'd attributed his survival to the botanical blend, which had indeed included quinine, along with gentian, caramel, dried orange zest, and other substances. His descendants had changed the recipe, lowered the alcohol content, and rendered the strange liqueur anodyne. Though small distilleries had stepped in to create approximations of the original over the years, Jude preferred to make her own. This batch was the last she'd produced, from back when you could still get oranges. She measured and poured.

Henri stirred. "What was that drink you made at Benedict's birthday party? That one really made me feel something."

"Degeneration Theory?" She smiled, then sighed: a surge of affection followed by a pressure wave of loss and despair. Oh, Benedict. He would have been better company than Henri, but even Henri was better than drinking alone. "That was a good party. It's not often you get to enact the downfall of civilization in microcosm in someone's living room."

"What are you making now? It's not . . . last call, is it?"

"Penultimate. This one's not entirely my own devising. It's called a Fin de Siècle."

Henri sat up and rested his jowly head in his hands. "Of course it is. End of the century. End of an era. Shouldn't we be in colonies on the moons of Jupiter by now? Or uploaded to quantum heaven?"

Jude ignored him. "This cocktail was popular in the 1890s. I think you'll enjoy it. Dry gin and bitter orange. The kind of complexity that lets you feel superior by liking it." Jude squinted at the trembling globe of fluid at the end of her dropper, then let it fall into the shaker. The bitters struck and dispersed in a radiating chaos of tendrils.

"What will this one make me feel?"

"What we should feel," she said. "Hopelessness. Exhaustion. They thought it was the end of civilization, in the 1890s. The slow collapse of the great human experiment."

"I could feel hopeless without your alchemy, Jude. I came here because I thought you could make this easier."

She shrugged, stirred the cocktail with a long-handled metal spoon, and then strained the concoction into a pair of long-stemmed glasses. "At least now you'll feel hopelessness while drinking a tasty cocktail. This will also rid you of a particular chemical poison that's probably causing you considerable pain."

"What's that?"

"Hope." She sat beside him on the love seat, wincing as she brushed away a clump of hair. She'd let the cat go yesterday; she couldn't be responsible for anything but herself anymore, and not even that for much longer.

"Here's to . . . everything." They clinked glasses.

"Shall we open the drapes?"

He shrugged, and she rose and pulled back the curtains, but didn't look through the glass until she'd returned to the couch. The views had always been exquisite, perched on the hillside here: you could see two bridges, the bay, the glinting towers of the Farallon arcology. The view was still glorious, from this vantage point, if viewed merely as an arrangement of light and form, without thought to the human consequences.

Henri gulped his drink, then coughed, spilling half the cocktail on his lap. "That is *bitter*."

"Look at the sky." She gestured with her glass. "Who knew it could be that color?"

"Who knew it could be that *shape*?" Henri had imbibed enough of her cocktail, and it was fast-acting enough, that he sank back into the couch and seemed to melt in on himself. "This is a suitable ending. We didn't even bring it on ourselves. It's just . . . happening."

Henri had been Benedict's friend, and then only out of habit.

"Maybe we are in a computer simulation, and all that out there is just . . . bit rot. Bad rendering." He glanced at her, hoping she'd be impressed, but Jude had heard a scientist make that same suggestion before the networks failed. Henri had never met an idea he wasn't happy to pass off as his own.

She put her nose on the rim of the glass and inhaled. Orange predominated. Hints of cucumber from the gin, along with the juniper and clove. She took a sip, and got all that and black pepper, too, along with the bitterness that made her choose this recipe. Henri slumped against her, and she didn't even mind, because nothing mattered. She couldn't tell if the color was really draining from the world or if that was an effect of her chemical wizardry. The overwhelming ennui, like being covered in a blanket of black mud, making all things gray. There were no more New Women. There was no more new anything. Even social degeneration implied an ongoing process, and this was the end of all that.

"May as well take the last drink." She lifted the flask she'd prepared earlier from the place where she'd wedged it between the cushions. "Do you want this in a glass?"

Henri didn't answer. He was crying. Interesting. Individual body chemistry always made the effects of her drugs somewhat unpredictable. He'd gotten the despair, and she'd been dosed with detachment. Or maybe he'd just spilled too much to experience the full effect. Oh well.

She tipped the fluid from the flask into her glass. She hadn't bothered to make this drink into art, but it picked up a bit of color from the dregs of her prior drink.

Last call tasted like nothing at all, which was just what she'd wanted. She let her chin fall onto her chest.

Henri sat up. "Jude." She squinted at him. His face was shiny in the light from the window, and the light was changing, softening his features, making them beautiful. "Look. The sky."

She looked up. The view had changed again. What had been a rending was now an opening; what had been a darkening a brightening; what had been a wall became a door.

End of an era, she thought, but there was no feeling attached to the thought. *A cycle ends. Another begins.*

Henri stood and walked to the window, his bulk blocking the view, which didn't please or upset her. "There's something coming through. I think . . . what if it's, what if it's different than we thought? Than everyone thought . . . Jude. Jude?"

She felt nothing at all. She closed her eyes to see it, too.

Fin de Siècle

I HESITATED TO INCLUDE THIS drink in this volume, but as it's one of my favorites, and is delicious, and very classy, I decided to go for it. My hesitation was centered on the difficulty of procuring one of the ingredients: Amer Picon, which is only commercially available in France—but in the end, it was the right choice to include it, if only because it inspired Mr. Pratt's delightful story.

Amer Picon is a fairly esoteric but crucial ingredient in the Fin de Siècle that falls into the category of "medicinal" bitters. Originally concocted by the scholar Gaétan Picon after contracting malaria whilst in Algeria, it contains quinine to guard against the disease. But, as Amer Picon is also delicious—it has strong quinine notes, but also tastes of orange and gentian—and was at the time very highly alcoholic for a liqueur, it quickly became a favorite in cocktails.

Given how bartenders and barflies alike are more interested in drier, bitter, more complicated flavors in cocktails, there's been a revival of drinks like the Fin de Siècle, which features Amer Picon—just a teaspoon, but that's enough to affect the drink. So, what's an aesthetic adventurer to do? Well, you can go to France and bring back a bottle. Or you can make your own Amer Picon—recipes exist on the Internet featuring fairly simple ways to home blend your own. Or you can get yourself a bottle of a wonderful American interpretation, the Amer Dit Picon from Golden Moon, a craft distillery in Colorado.

Ingredients
1½ oz. London dry gin
¾ oz. Italian sweet vermouth
¼ oz. Amer Picon
Several dashes of orange bitters

How to Make it: Once you've procured your Amer Picon or surrogate, pour all ingredients into a shaker, stir with lots of ice until very cold, then strain into a coupe. No garnish needed!

Henry Wotton

AMED FOR THE LOUCHE ARISTOCRAT from Oscar Wilde's *Picture of Dorian Gray*, the Henry Wotton is a drink based solely off a light description of a beverage its namesake enjoys in the novel: "'Oh, she is more than good—she is beautiful,' murmured Lord Henry, sipping a glass of vermouth and orange-bitters." I tried it on a lark, but it's actually quite lovely when you do it up right, with top-shelf vermouth (of which there are increasingly more these days, thank the Maker). I usually stick with Punt e Mes, given its cost-to-deliciousness ratio, but as long as you avoid the nastiest of your local liquor store's offerings you'll be fine. I usually have Fee Bros. orange bitters lying around, and they're perfectly grand, but I'm sure you could go fancier on that, too.

Ingredients
2 oz. sweet Italian vermouth
Orange bitters
Orange twist, to garnish

How to Make It: The drink is ridiculously simple—in a cocktail shaker, measure out the vermouth and lace liberally with orange bitters. Stir with cracked ice and strain into a chilled cocktail glass. Garnish with an orange twist. It's essential to get this drink very cold indeed, so if you're not in the habit of keeping your vermouth in the fridge, go on and chill it. (You should be keeping your vermouth in the fridge anyway, to preserve it for longer.)

Arrangement in Juniper and Champagne

by Selena Chambers

I T WAS *ARRANGEMENT IN JUNIPER and Champagne* that prompted Ansley and Luce to move beyond basic conversational niceties. An explosion of newspaper and glue typical of the Berlin Dada photomontages, this one stood out from the other pieces in the *Pa-PeRcUtS* exhibit thanks to its anonymity, and to its juxtaposition of café society with the wartime trenches. Bottles of Gordon's Gin and Moët & Chandon champagne interchanged with flirting flappers and wooing bureaucrats over a bistro table attached to a French 75 mm field gun. From the cannon: lemons, spermatozoa, bullets, and embryos scattered into the foreground and background, and from some fourth dimensional plane conjured by the artist a group of German skeletal soldiers collapsed together into fetal slouches like a line of fallen dominoes. The last in line gestured defense with rigor mortis hands. In his left palm dangled a découpaged champagne coupé identical to those held by the revelers in the visual tornado above him.

"What's the German say?" Ansley asked Luce, gesturing at the label on the wall next to *Arrangement in Juniper and Champagne*.

"The description says, 'Past is past. Present is present. The future is always tenable.' It also says they think it might be by Hannah Höch, but that hasn't been verified. I don't know. It seems too . . ."

"Heavy-handed?" said Ansley.

"Well, I was gonna say 'literal.'"

Ansley stuck her nose close to the glass. "I don't get it."

"What's there to get? Once knocked up by the Republic, always knocked up by the Republic." Luce smiled over her shoulder at Ansley, but found her gone to the middle of the gallery, collapsed onto the bench like one of the collage's trench-sons. Luce gave *Arrangement in Juniper and Champagne* one last glance, then joined her friend.

"You okay?" Luce asked. Ansley looked past her, returning her gaze to the photomontage.

"I'm fine. Just kind of tired."

"Ah, I've got just the thing." Luce fished inside her blazer and withdrew a brown leather bound flask. "They always check the purses; they *never* check the pockets."

Luce swayed the flask in front of Ansley's face, now flushed and set in bitch mode.

"You'll never guess what's in here." Luce cut her eyes toward the collage.

"French 75?"

"Good guess."

"Hmm."

"I thought you'd be excited. You used to love public drinking."

"Yeah, when I was twenty-two," Ansley said.

"Was twenty-two so long ago?"

"Believe me, it's ancient history. The two years you've been gone—also ancient history. And, meanwhile, some of us have had to grow up."

"I wouldn't say you *had* to, Mom," Luce said.

"Don't call me that." Ansley raised her voice. "I hear that enough from my actual kids as it is."

Luce tucked the flask into her blazer just as a docent entered the gallery. He scowled at them as he passed, then strode into the next gallery.

Luce brought the flask back out and unscrewed it. The top sprung back with a small pop, and cocktail spilled onto Ansley's lap. She grabbed Ansley before she could jump up.

"I'm sorry." She giggled. "I'm sorry. It's the champagne." Ansley sniffed the astringent bouquet of lemons, cucumber gin, and fermented grapes.

"Great, now the docent is going to smell it!"

"Are you seriously afraid that guy's paid enough to give a shit? Just sit . . . play cool." She dabbed at Ansley's skirt with her sleeve. "See, we'll share the shame."

Luce wiped the sides of the flask onto her jeans, then raised it up in the air.

"It's great to see you again, Ansley." She quaffed, then offered the flask. "Come on, Ans. Have a drink with me. It's good—I swear. I mean, it's not like what you get at Harry's New York in Paris, but—"

"I wouldn't know the difference." Ansley turned away from Luce to regard the collage again. Luce shrugged and took another swig.

"You know, speaking of Harry's . . . I went there my first night, and it was full of Americans, like you'd expect—"

"You went by yourself?"

"Of course I did. Just listen, though, this is funny—"

"Did you meet anyone?"

"At Harry's?"

"I mean, over the last two years."

"No, not really." Luce punctuated her utterance with another swig. Ansley made a face. "So, anyway, at Harry's, this couple came in—"

"Don't you feel like you're missing out?"

"On what?"

"Kids! I know in college you swore to never —"

"I did," Luce said, "and so did you."

"Yeah, well, I didn't mean it," Ansley said.

"Well, that's why I never shot you for it."

"What do you mean?"

"You don't remember our pact?"

"That if either of us ever gave up our dreams for the so-called 'good life', the other would shoot her right in the head?" Ansley said. "That wasn't literal."

"Obviously not," Luce said. "I always imagined it as a form of public embarrassment. Even so, I meant it figuratively, but you didn't mean it at all. So, I didn't shoot you at your wedding, and I didn't shoot you when your crotch-goblins were born."

"You weren't even here for any of that!"

"You're right. I wasn't there for any of those things, and I'm sorry. But, even if I had been, Ans, what would it have mattered? It wouldn't have changed anything."

"It does matter. It matters now."

Luce wrapped her arm around Ansley's shoulder.

"Shhh. Do you want the docent to think that you're drunk?" Ansley swallowed a sob.

"I'm not drunk." She sighed inside her palms.

"And therein lies your problem."

Ansley raised her head and saw Luce waggling the flask.

"True, but I can't, Luce. I can't fucking drink alcohol, right now . . . because I *can't*."

"Oh."

"Yeah."

"Oh, shit." Luce secured the flask and returned it to her blazer's interior pocket. "Again?"

Ansley put her face in her hands and began sobbing. Luce wrapped her arm around Ansley's shoulder.

"I can't do this again. I don't want to be a baby field gun for the Republic!"

"Who said you were?"

"You. You and that terrible Hannah Höch wannabe!"

"I . . . didn't . . ."

"That's what you think of me, anyway. Your face says it all!"

"My face! Your face said I had cancer when I said I didn't have a boyfriend." Ansley began sobbing again.

"Does Dan know yet?"

Ansley shook her head. "I did the pee stick this morning."

"Well, then," Luce said, "you have time to figure out what you really want. There are always options—tenable futures, according to that wannabe Höch on the wall."

Ansley shrugged free of Luce's embrace. She stood up and straightened her cocktail-soaked skirt and returned to the collage. Luce took another swig from the flask while watching Ansley, savoring the spiked lemonade bubbling down her throat. She checked her phone and noticed that the gallery was about to close. She stood up and went to Ansley.

"I get it now."

Ansley held out her hand.

"Get what?" Luce said.

"Shoot me."

"What?"

"Give me the flask," she hissed.

"Ans . . . I don't think—"

"You brought the artillery—now use it. Shoot me." The docent poked his head in.

"We are closing in two minutes, ladies."

Luce slipped the hand holding the flask behind her back. "Right behind you, sir!" she called out to him. Ansley regarded *Arrangement in Juniper and Champagne* a final time and tugged the flask free from Luce's hand.

"It was good to see you again, Luce," she said. Then she smiled, lifted the flask to her lips, and drained it dry.

French 75

LEMONY DRINKS ARE THE MOST contentious when it comes to determining the One True Recipe it seems, now that I think about it. Anyway, so, the French 75! Named for a gun that might be small but packs a wallop, this drink calls to mind Jazz Age parties and deeply terrible hangovers. Let's focus on the former while concocting my sweeter, lighter version of this classic.

I love the taste of champagne so I reduce just about everything in my recipe so everything is balanced, at least to my palate. As always, concoct to your own taste, but I think my version is a good place to start. Plus it fits in a standard flute with enough room for a goodly tot of champagne; you really need a Collins glass if you're going to do one up with an entire ounce of lemon, two of gin, plus simple syrup, etc. Some people like to make weird specifications about the length of the lemon garnish, but while I'm all for tradition, I'm not going to get the tape measure out to ensure my peels are all five inches long or what have you. Thin enough to be pretty, long enough to get a bit of lemon oil on the surface will do the drink just fine.

Ingredients

1 oz. gin

½ oz. fresh lemon juice

1 tbsp. simple syrup

Brut champagne

Lemon twist, to garnish

How to Make It: Shake gin, lemon juice, and the simple syrup in a shaker with lots of ice. Pour into a champagne flute and top with the bubbly. Garnish with a long, thin twist of lemon peel.

Simple syrup really is simple: it's equal proportions sugar and water, heated up to dissolve the sugar, and cooled. Store it up to a month in your fridge, preferably in a glass container, as plastic stuff can impart off-flavors. You don't have to limit its use to cocktails, either; use it to sweeten iced teas and coffees, or in desserts like ice cream to get a silkier texture. You can also flavor it with citrus peel, herbs, or spices—put them in at the end after you take it off the heat. If you flavor your simple syrups, use those faster—within a week or so.

Most liquor stores sell simple syrup, but you're really just paying them to package it and ship it to you. DIY!

There and Back Again

by Carmen Maria Machado

MY MOTHER USED TO LOVE the corpse reviver. She called it the perfect cocktail. "The thing that sends you away, brings you back," she'd say as she laid out the ingredients on the dining room table before she went out for the evening. "There is only one door," she clarified once, when I looked at her in confusion. "You can go out and you can come in, but you always have to pass through the same door to get there."

I was too young to understand hair-of-the-dog as a concept, much less as an idiom, but there was some sort of clear alchemy happening on that table: the martini glass clear of smudges, the burnished aluminum shaker, the arrangement of bottles and their mysterious liquids, deep red maraschino cherries floating in a pickling jar at the end of the row. It was understood that I was not to touch this arrangement ("None of this is for little girls"), and she would know: my fingerprints on the glass would give me away. This didn't stop me from inverting the jar to watch the cherries rise like so many jellyfish, and then wiping it clean on my nightgown. But I'd only do that after she left.

And she did leave, once a week. A kiss dropped somewhere in my hair, and she'd walk out the front door and into the humid, mottled darkness.

I'd wait for her. The house felt strange when she was gone; like it'd been shucked from the thing that gave it purpose. The air hummed with her many ghosts: skin cells, perfume, the cobwebs she'd ignored from when we first moved in. I listened for hours for the sound of tires, of the front door opening, of her inky voice exchanging murmurs with a stranger.

The men and women she brought home were beautiful. The women were always dark-haired and curvy—her type. The men looked like they'd been dragged through a dewy meadow. My mother would always offer them a drink, then she'd walk past the stairs to see if I was waiting. Then her footsteps would cut a path toward the kitchen.

"On the rocks?" she'd call. My cue. I'd step into the living room and walk slowly to the body, slumped loosely on the love seat. Their gaze was always focused on the kitchen doorway through which my mother had disappeared. I could feel them listening to the comforting sounds of ice striking glass, hope stirring through the haze of alcohol.

They were easy to eat when they were like that. Soft. Fermented, almost. And when I was done, she would collect me and take me upstairs, and we would sleep two heavy, parallel sleeps: her besotted with alcohol, me with blood and bone. The next morning, I'd always find her sitting at the table, rolling a silky glaze of absinthe around the inside of the martini glass and staring at the place where the sunlight struck the floorboards.

It was that way for many years, the two of us. And then she died and I was alone.

* * *

Learning to feed myself was hard. I've never been good with people. Perhaps that seems like a bit of a joke, but I imagine it's how certain men see the world, too: if all you want is a body, it's difficult to confront the animated spirit within.

Even when I wasn't hungry—even when I'd just eaten—it was hard to focus on the ethereal, flickering qualities that made humans individual: a smile, for example, or a voice. They were like crows—I'd been told of their intelligence, their distinctiveness, but couldn't quite bring myself to believe it.

So I was lucky that I was beautiful, that people let me come home with them even after I'd spent a date barely looking them in the eye. Which is how, a year after my mother died, I ended up at Alma's place.

I didn't mean to follow her home. That is, I tried to invite her to my place, but she'd sweetly refused, and I found myself paying closer attention to her than I had to anyone in a very long time.

"My house is closer," I said.

She smiled shyly and shook her head. I hadn't been drinking much, but she had, and every tip of her—nose, ears, cheekbones—were slightly flushed. "I'd just feel better if we were at my place," she said. "More, um, comfortable?"

In the cab she sat close to me, and a few blocks from the bar she opened up my fist—I didn't know I'd been making a fist—and gently stroked her fingers over my palm. The sensation was so intimate I nearly threw myself out the door and into the street, but then we were in front of her building, and then we were upstairs, and she sat me down on the couch by clumsily pressing both hands on my shoulders. I was still unnerved from the feeling of her fingers in my palm; I so rarely touched people with anything but my teeth, my throat.

The apartment had a curio-cabinet charm, with stone figurines and candles and intricate, draped fabrics. A preserved crocodile head sat on the bookshelf, and the smell of incense—familiar, somehow—lingered in the air. She came out of the kitchen with something amber-gold in a tumbler. I started; I'd been planning on doing it when she'd been there, but I'd been distracted. I couldn't remember the last time I'd lost focus like this. As a child, maybe.

I drank deeply. I hated seeing this apartment, the corners and tendrils of her life. I wanted to eat and then I wanted to leave.

"I hope this is all right," she said. "The drink, I mean. I didn't mean to assume, I just—I don't do this very much. Well, ever."

"It's fine. I mean, it's good. My mom used to make really complicated cocktails when I was a kid, and I took secret sips out of a few of them. Never liked them much. This is easier."

"What would she make?"

"Um, there was this one called a corpse reviver. Like, a hair-of-the-dog cocktail? Just, lots of booze with a cherry dropped in. Oh, and you had to coat the glass with absinthe, first. Really complicated. I don't even know where she learned it."

I drained my glass to the ice and set it down into darkness.

* * *

When I opened my eyes again, the ceiling rocked gently above me, like a boat bobbing against the tide. Alma's face swam into view.

"I didn't actually know if that would work," she said. "But there you are." She stood up and stepped over me, and her voice sounded like it was coming from the end of a long tunnel. "Do you know who I am?"

I struggled to make words. "G-girlfriend of a missing person."

"Good guess," she said. "Sister of a missing person."

He'd had the smell of incense on his clothes. I remembered now. He'd been early on, when I talked to them too much, learned too much. I didn't remember his name, but he'd talked about his older sister, whom he adored.

"He was living with me," Alma said. "Trying to get his life back on track after a bad breakup. Lonely, you know? Wanted to go on some dates. And then he went out one night and never came back."

"Loneliness is a door," I said. "You—"

I turned and retched over the carpet.

"You look like an animal," she said.

"Loneliness is a door," I said again. "You can go out and you can come in, but you always have to pass through loneliness to get there."

"What do I have to do?" she said. "Stake through the heart? Silver bullet? What the hell are you? Where is his body?"

"What sends you away will bring you back," I said. "I ate your brother. Every part of him."

"Do I have to eat you?" she said. Her voice was low and sad.

"Hunger is a door. You can go out and you can come in, but you always have to pass through hunger to get there."

She knelt down over me. She was holding a chef's knife in her hand, both of which were trembling. "I just want my brother back."

I grabbed her shirt and pulled her down close to my face. Through my disorientation, I opened my mouth wide enough, so she could see. So she could really see.

"Vengeance is a door," I said, my voice rippling through cities of teeth, forests of muscle, miles of esophagus. "You can go out and you can come in, but you always have to pass through vengeance to get there." I reached up and circled the knife's blade with my hand. "So pick your door."

* * *

She left me, alive, in an alley in a neighboring city, upright next to a dumpster. "There are always windows," she said as she got back into her car, but I couldn't tell if she was talking to herself, or to me.

Corpse Reviver #2

THIS IS THE DRINK THAT started it all for your humble cocktail editrix. When I'm not writing effortlessly sophisticated cocktail copy, I write literary horror and fantasy short stories and novels, and it was at a World Horror Convention in Austin, Texas, where I first got into cocktails. A bar there, Péché, enchanted me with its Fin de Siècle charm and pre-Prohibition cocktails. As it was *à la mode*, I ordered this ghostly-sounding concoction and was rewarded with a cocktail unlike any I'd ordered before. Sweet, lemony, balanced, luscious, intoxicating—a meal of a cocktail, and one served with its own dessert: a brandied cherry in the bottom. Perfect.

When I got home, I immediately set to recreating it, and after learning that Lillet Blanc has changed its recipe over the years, eventually settled on these proportions as the ideal version of the drink. It's a recipe lighter on the lemon than many, as I don't like a cocktail that is too tart, and since only recently have I actually designated a little bottle with an eye dropper specifically to absinthe, I've given you my "hack" as the kids say, of using a scant teaspoon instead of the traditional eight drops.

Ingredients

1½ oz. Lillet Blanc

1½ oz. London dry gin

½ oz. lemon juice

¾ oz. Cointreau

8 drops absinthe (about 1 scant teaspoon)

Brandied cherry

How to Make It: In a cocktail shaker, combine the above ingredients sans cherry and shake vigorously with lots of cracked ice until very cold. I like to put the cherry in the bottom of a large chilled cocktail glass and then add a bit of the syrup atop it, then pour what should be a very light, cloudy, lemon-colored cocktail slowly down the side of the glass to not disturb the more viscous cherry syrup, creating a nice layering effect. Serve and drink cold, and don't linger over this one.

Appendix: Setting Up Your Bar

• •

I DIDN'T FOLLOW ANY SORT of guide like this when I first became interested in home cocktail mixing. Maybe I should have, but the truth is, I started out by using what I had, and over time bought a few more esoteric ingredients and tools that made my life much easier and my cocktails much tastier. But, given that these days there are ten thousand guides out there by this or that home mixologist or famous bartender recommending all sorts of weird things— eyedroppers for absinthe or bitters; little mist-producing appliances that spray vermouth over the surface of a drink—I figured it would be keeping with the spirit (get it?) of the recipe section of the book to talk about what you really need, and what you really don't, to make great drinks at home.

Spirits

It's all about what you like, and what you think you'll make frequently. That might sound general and unhelpful, but if neither you nor any of your close friends enjoy tequila, why keep it in the house? Anyway, if you really want a "fully stocked" home bar, I'd suggest always keeping on hand decent versions of the following: gin, vodka, silver and golden rum, tequila, and bourbon and/or rye whiskey. In order to keep a stocked bar without breaking the bank I usually watch the sales at my local stores—stuff like rum and gin go on sale during the winter; bourbon in the summer. The stuff doesn't go bad, so go on and think ahead.

Going beyond base spirits, I almost always have the following on hand: Cointreau, a real absinthe, high-quality dry and sweet vermouth, Lillet Blanc, Campari, maraschino liqueur, and some sort of decent brandy or cognac. (This is also a decent guide to what you'll need to make the drinks in this book, though there are some exceptions.) Not sure if you'll like an ingredient you see listed in a recipe here or in another cocktail book some other mild acquaintance got you last Christmas? Ask for a shot of it at a bar the next time you're out and about, or ask for a drink to be made with it, to see if you think it plays well with others. That's how I first tried Cynar, a delicious amaro (bitter liqueur) that I was skeptical of, given that it claims to contain artichokes. Indeed I found it delicious, and I've kept it in the house ever since.

Bells and Whistles

A good home bartender will try to always have a few limes, lemons, and oranges in the crisper. That way, your bases are covered for just about anything you'd care to make, whenever the mood strikes you. I'd also recommend keeping a jar of green olives in the fridge, alongside a jar of real brandied cherries. Not maraschino cherries, like you'd put on a child's sundae—the real deal, made with real booze, that you'll buy in the liquor store for what will seem like a lot of money. (NB: when you pick up that 18-dollar jar of cherries, just do what I do and whisper to yourself, *You're worth it.* I mean, really, how many jars do you expect to go through in a year? Go for it. You're worth it.) I also always keep sugar cubes in the house—that might seem exotic, but they're in any major grocery store's baking aisle—and bitters. If you're new to the mixological arts, and are using this guide to upgrade from only having a bottle of Fireball Whiskey in the house from that time your college roommate needed a place to crash, invest in a bottle of Angostura aromatic bitters, and a bottle of orange bitters. Those are the salt and pepper of home bartending. The other, fancier stuff—smoked orange, bourbon barrel, rhubarb, grapefruit, chocolate—can wait until you need 'em, or get curious.

Equipment

You could spend a fortune outfitting a home bar, but that's unnecessary. A few simple pieces of equipment will set you up for just about any recipe. If you get into home bartending, upgrade as needed—I recently, *finally* bought myself a muddler, instead of using the handle of a wooden spoon—so you can usually get by without anything too fancy.

Essential

A shaker, either cobbler or Boston. Cobbler shakers are the kind with three parts—a cup, a strainer with a spout, and a lid. That's what I use. A Boston shaker is basically a pint glass with a metal cup. They're very impressive to watch someone else use, but I don't care for them. I don't care if the lid of your Cobbler has a jigger built-in, as mine does, get a real jigger. I have two—a two-ounce jigger, and one that has the standard one-and-a-half to three-quarter ounce measure. I consider both essential, but most people get by with the latter. You can eyeball that extra half-ounce. I also consider a vegetable peeler (for rinds) and measuring spoons essential, but most people already own those. No need to get a separate set. Finally, I'm going to put an ice crusher on this list of essentials. I know it doesn't seem that way, but crushed ice really is crucial for juleps, and it makes it so much easier to get cocktails cold quickly. If you have an ice crusher in your fridge, don't worry about it; if not, grab one. They're not expensive online, and that way you'll never smash your thumb banging a zip-top bag of ice cubes with a rolling pin.

Good to Have

A Hawthorne strainer. Those are the ones with the little wire coil. For cocktails that are stirred, not shaken, they're nice to have—though you can of course use the strainer of your cobbler, which is what I usually do when I'm home with my cat. He doesn't judge me. A bar spoon is also nice, but take it from me, you can just use a chopstick. Put one on your Amazon.com wish list or wedding registry; don't fret about going out and getting a spoon right away. Same with a muddler—you can just use the handle of a wooden spoon. A channel knife can be cool for fiddly thin bits of peel like you'd put in a French 75 or Vesper, but I don't own one. I'll get around to it eventually. Probably. I do have a designated citrus knife and cutting board, just because I'm lazy and I never need to worry about my Sangria apples picking up essence of onion.

Glasses

Barware is pretty cheap these days at big-box stores, so go on and pick up a few of the following glasses:

- **Cocktail, aka Martini.** I mean, you're mixing cocktails, aren't you?
- **Coupe.** A more rounded, bowl-like cocktail glass; I like them because they're less tippy and they give a bit of old-fashioned flair to drinks like the Fin de Siècle.
- **Old Fashioned.** Sometimes called a lowball or rocks glass, old fashioned glasses have a thick bottom so you can mash and muddle right in the cup itself. I personally don't have metal julep cups so I use old fashioned glasses for many of the drinks in this book.
- **Collins or Highball.** You could get both if you want. Collins glasses are taller and thinner; highball are wider and lower, but still higher than an old fashioned glass. Truth be told my motley cabinet of glassware has a few of each, remnants from sets I've broken most of over the years.
- **Champagne flutes and wineglasses.** You know, to drink your champagne cocktails and sangria out of.

Follow the above instructions, and you'll be set up for most home bartending. You'll also be set up because if you actually buy all the above, your friends will definitely think to themselves, "Gosh, so-and-so is super into cocktail stuff!" and buy you books like this one, plus fancier bar equipment than you need come your birthday or the holiday season.

Contributor Biographies

The Editors:

Nick Mamatas is the author of several novels, including *I Am Providence* and *Hexen Sabbath*. His short fiction and essays have appeared in *Best American Mystery Stories*, *Asimov's Science Fiction*, *New Haven Review*, the *Village Voice*, *Poets and Writers*, and many other venues. As an anthologist, he coedited the Bram Stoker Award-winning *Haunted Legends* with Ellen Datlow, and the Locus Award nominees *The Future is Japanese* and *Hanzai Japan* with Masumi Washington.

Molly Tanzer is the author of the novels *Creatures of Will and Temper*, *Vermilion*, and *The Pleasure Merchant*, and the British Fantasy and Wonderland Book Award-nominated collection-cum-mosaic novel *A Pretty Mouth*. Her short fiction has appeared in *Lightspeed Magazine*, *Nightmare Magazine*, and *Transcendent: The Year's Best Transgender and Genderqueer Speculative Fiction*, as well as many other locations. Her other editorial projects include being the editrix of *Congress Magazine*, which publishes thoughtful erotica. She lives in Longmont, Colorado.

The Contributors:

Maurice Broaddus is the author of *The Knights of Breton Court* urban fantasy trilogy. Published in such venues as *Asimov's Science*

Fiction, *Lightspeed Magazine*, *Cemetery Dance*, *Apex Magazine*, and *Weird Tales Magazine*, some of his stories have been collected in *The Voices of Martyrs*. He also coedited the *Streets of Shadows* and the *Dark Faith* anthology series. You can keep up with him at his website, www.MauriceBroaddus.com.

Selena Chambers is a Hugo and World Fantasy Award-nominated editor, author, and Floridian. Her latest projects include a debut short story collection, *Calls for Submission*, from Pelekinesis and a forthcoming crossed-genre anthology, *Mechanical Animals*, coedited with Hugo winner Jason Heller, released by Hex Publishing in 2018. To learn more about Selena and her work, please visit www.selenachambers.com.

Libby Cudmore is the author of *The Big Rewind*, which received a starred review from Kirkus, as well as praise from *USA Today*, *Publishers Weekly*, *Booklist*, and others. Her short fiction and essays have appeared in *PANK, The Stoneslide Corrective, Beat to a Pulp, Vinyl Me Please, Yacht Rock*, and the Locus Award-nominated anthology *Hanzai Japan*.

Gina Marie Guadagnino holds a BA in English from NYU, and an MFA in Creative Writing from the New School. Her short story "Whisper in the Shadows" appears in *The Morris-Jumel Mansion Anthology of Fantasy and Paranormal Fiction*.

Elizabeth Hand is the author of numerous award-winning novels and four collections of short fiction. Her reviews and essays have appeared in the *Los Angeles Times*, *Washington Post*, *Boston Review*, and

Salon, among many others. She divides her time between the coast of Maine and North London.

Cara Hoffman is the author of the critically acclaimed novels *Running* and *So Much Pretty*. She is the recipient of numerous awards and accolades, including a Folio Prize nomination and a Sundance Institute Global Filmmaking Award. She has written for the *New York Times*, *Marie Claire*, *Salon*, and *National Public Radio*, and has been a visiting writer at the University of Oxford. She is currently a professor at University of Southern Maine's Stonecoast MFA program.

Jarett Kobek is a Turkish-American author living in California. His self-published novel *I Hate the Internet* has been an international bestseller and appeared in seven languages.

Carrie Laben earned her MFA at the University of Montana. Her work has appeared in such venues as *Indiana Review*, *The Dark*, *Okey-Panky*, and *The Year's Best Dark Fantasy and Horror*. She has twice been nominated for the Shirley Jackson Award, and in 2015 was selected for the Anne LaBastille Memorial Writer's Residency.

Carmen Maria Machado is the author of *Her Body and Other Parties*. Her writing has appeared in *The New Yorker*, *Granta*, *Best American Science Fiction & Fantasy*, *Best Horror of the Year*, and elsewhere, and her story "The Husband Stitch" was nominated for the Nebula and Shirley Jackson Awards. She holds an MFA from the Iowa Writers' Workshop and lives in Philadelphia with her wife.

Jim Nisbet has published twenty books, including *Lethal Injection*, widely regarded as a classic *roman noir*; six volumes of poetry, most recently *Sonnets*; and a single nonfiction title, *Laminating The Conic Frustum*. Current projects include his fourteenth novel, *You Don't Pencil*, and a complete translation of *Les Fleurs du Mal*.

Benjamin Percy's most recent novel is *The Dark Net*. He writes the *Green Arrow* and *Teen Titans* series for DC Comics, and *James Bond* for Dynamite Entertainment. His honors include an NEA fellowship, the Whiting Writers' Award, the Plimpton Prize, two Pushcart Prizes, and inclusion in *Best American Short Stories* and *Best American Comics*.

Dominica Phetteplace writes literary and science fiction. Her work has appeared in *Asimov's Science Fiction*, *The Magazine of Fantasy and Science Fiction*, *Clarkesworld*, *PANK*, and *The Los Angeles Review*. She has won a Barbara Deming Award, a Pushcart Prize, and fellowships from the MacDowell Colony, I-Park, and the Steinbeck Fellows Program of San José State University.

Tim Pratt is the author of over twenty novels, with his newest book, space opera *The Wrong Stars*. His stories have appeared in *Best American Short Stories*, *The Year's Best Fantasy*, *The Mammoth Book of Best New Horror*, and other nice places. He's a Hugo Award winner, and has been a finalist for World Fantasy, Sturgeon, Stoker, Mythopoeic, and Nebula Awards, among others. Every month he writes a new story for his Patreon supporters at www.patreon.com/timpratt.

Robert Swartwood is the *USA Today* bestselling author of over ten novels, including *The Serial Killer's Wife*, *Man of Wax*, and *No Shelter*.

He created the term "hint fiction" and is the editor of *Hint Fiction: An Anthology of Stories in 25 Words or Fewer*. He lives with his wife in Pennsylvania.

Jeff VanderMeer's novels include the Southern Reach trilogy (*Annihilation*, *Authority*, and *Acceptance*), which have been translated into 35 languages. A past winner of the Nebula Award, World Fantasy Award, and Shirley Jackson Award, VanderMeer also writes nonfiction for *The Guardian*, *Los Angeles Times*, *New York Times Book Review*, and many others. He is the coeditor with his wife, Ann VanderMeer, of *The Big Book of Science Fiction* and *The Weird*.

Will Viharo is the author of *The Thrillville Pulp Fiction Collection* Volumes 1–3, the erotic horror novella *Things I Do When I'm Awake*, the Vic Valentine, Private Eye series, and two science fiction novels with Scott Fulks, *It Came from Hangar 18* and *The Space Needler's Intergalactic Bar Guide*. He writes a regular movie column for *Bachelor Pad Magazine* and is the host and organizer of Noir at the Bar Seattle.